MAYBE I WILL

LAURIE GRAY

LUMINIS BOOKS

LUMINIS BOOKS
Published by Luminis Books
1950 East Greyhound Pass, #18, PMB 280,
Carmel, Indiana, 46033, U.S.A.
Copyright © Socratic Parenting LLC, 2013

Grateful acknowledgment is made to Hal Leonard Corporation for permission to quote from the songs "I've Gotta Crow" © 1954 (Renewed) Carolyn Leigh and Mark Charlap and "Ugg-A-Wugg" © 1954 (Renewed) Betty Comden, Adolph Green, and Jule Styne from PETER PAN, All Rights Controlled by Edwin H. Morris and Company, a Division of MPL Music Publishing, Inc. All rights reserved. Used by permission.

Chapter 9 reference: *Shakespeare: The Complete Works*. Ed. G. B. Harrison. New York: Harcourt, 1968.

The author is grateful to the American Taekwondo Association for its empowering programs and for granting permission to use the ATA pledge in this work.

Hardcover: 978-1-935462-71-2
Paperback: 978-1-935462-70-5

Printed in the United States of America

10 9 8 7 6 5 4 3 2 1

Advance praise for *Maybe I Will*:

In *Maybe I Will*, author Laurie Gray deals with a difficult topic in a thoughtful, nuanced, and realistic way. A pinch of humor and a dash of Shakespeare add flavor to what otherwise might be an overly heavy stew.

Maybe I Will belongs on teens' reading lists and bookshelves alongside classics of its type such as Laurie Halse Anderson's *Speak* and Cheryl Rainfield's *Scars*.

—Mike Mullin, award-winning author of *Ashfall* and *Ashen Winter*

When a young person changes, suddenly and dramatically, there may be a reason that is not immediately apparent. In *Maybe I Will*, Laurie Gray insightfully explores such a situation. You will want to read this story twice.

—Helen Frost, Printz Honor Award-winning author of *Keesha's House*

Maybe I Will is an essential purchase for libraries with young adults requesting books like *13 Reasons Why* by Jay Asher, *The Rules of Survival* by Nancy Werlin, and *Speak* by Laurie Halse Anderson.

We never know for sure if the victim is a boy or a girl. Pulling that perspective off was a dramatic success. By having the character almost gender neutral, this title will be easier to put in both male and female reader's hands.

Maybe I Will may be the title that helps a teen open up and tell someone, rather than continue to suffer in silence.

—Practically Paradise — Diane R. Kelly

*This book is dedicated to Michelle Ditton
and all of the Sexual Assault Nurse Examiners
who helped me understand that
it's not about sex.*

MAYBE I WILL

Prologue

MY PARENTS STARTED calling me Sandy the night they conceived me. I've heard the story hundreds of times. It's their fifth anniversary, and they're on the beach under a billion stars. Mom just made partner at her law firm, and Dad just finished his doctoral thesis on Shakespeare.

Mom asks, "What would you like for our anniversary?"

So Dad says, "Let's make a baby."

(Fast forward through the rolling in sand part.)

Mom sighs and says, "I think we did it."

"A little sandy, don't you think?"

Mom nods. "Sanford or Sandra?"

And Dad says, "Yes."

He pops the cork on a bottle of champagne, and they toast, "To Sandy Peareson."

1

All the world's a stage,
And all the men and women merely players.
They all have their exits and their entrances,
And one man in his time plays many parts…

—*As You Like It*, Act II, Scene vii, Lines 139-142

MY FOURTH BIRTHDAY fell on a Friday during my sophomore year of high school. If I looked four, maybe I could have passed for a child prodigy. Only my birthday was February 29th, so really it took me 16 years to get to my fourth birthday. It used to make me crazy—how the whole world could just skip my birthday three years in a row. No one else I knew was born on Leap Year.

Since it would really, truly be my birthday that Friday, and I hadn't had an honest-to-god birthday since I was 12, I felt like all the gods were smiling on me, and I could have anything I really wanted. What I really wanted was to go to Juilliard, but it was still a little early for that. I'd have to settle for the lead in our school spring musical. Tryouts were scheduled for Friday, February 29. The musical was *Peter Pan,* so there were three major roles—Peter Pan, Wendy, and Captain Hook—and I'd been thinking that with all the makeup and costumes and stuff, I could play any one of them.

That's why I called a "Meeting of the Minds" with Cassie and Troy when they picked me up for school that Thursday morning. I wanted them to give me the latest on who was trying out for what parts and all. The great thing about our friendship was that we each had our own things we did best. We hadn't competed for anything since we were potty trained. No kidding. Cassie's mom babysat me and Troy every day and ended up potty training all three of us. That's probably why Cassie won. Consistency, 24-7.

Cassie's mom used to put us in one of those strollers that hold three kids with Cassie in front (even then Cassie needed a little distance from her mom), me in the middle, and Troy in the back closest to her because Troy didn't have a mom and wanted to be close to any mom whenever he could.

So every day Cassie's mom would push us like that all over the university campus. It didn't matter how hot it was or how cold it was, as long as there wasn't some sort of blizzard or lightning storm or tornado, she pushed us around the dorms, through the student union and past the English department where my dad taught.

Cassie was the first one to ditch the stroller. Dad says he was teaching *The Tempest*, Act V, Scene i:

A devil, a born devil, on whose nature
Nurture can never stick, on whom my pains,
Humanely taken, all, all lost, quite lost.

He looked out the window and saw Cassie standing in the front seat of the stroller looking like Washington crossing the Delaware.

I guess Troy and I still hadn't figured out how to unbuckle the seatbelts. Anyway, Cassie's mom freaked out and ran around to the front of the stroller to hook Cassie back in. Only she forgot to set the brake on the stroller and when she ran forward, we rolled backward with Cassie's mom chasing after us, arms outstretched yelling, "Cassie! Stop! Cassie!" Cassie swore she never trusted her mom since and that her mom would forever blame Troy and me for pulling Cassie away from her. The lady doth protest too much. That's *Hamlet*, Act III, Scene ii.

So, back to that Thursday morning. When Cassie leaned her head out of the passenger side of Troy's white Monte Carlo and called to me on my front steps. "Hey, Sandy! What's Shakin'?" I replied, "When shall we three meet again? In thunder, lightning or in rain?" Those are the opening lines of *Macbeth*. Troy and Cassie always asked me "What's Shakin'?" They thought I was obsessed with all things related to the Bard. At first, they were just ribbing me, but now it's sort of our thing. I try to answer them with a quote from Shakespeare. "When shall we three meet again..." meant I was calling a Meeting of the Minds.

Nobody had called a Meeting of the Minds since Troy's birthday last summer. Cassie and Troy had this pact since sixth grade that Cassie would have sex with Troy on his 16th birthday if he was still a virgin. Troy always had this huge crush on Cassie. And Cassie… well, everybody but Troy knew that he just was not Cassie's type. But Troy saved himself for Cassie, and she kept her word.

Afterward Troy kept telling Cassie how much he loved her and begging her to go with him, which just totally freaked Cassie out. That wasn't part of the deal. And then when her pigskin prince went off to college and ditched her, Cassie had this thing about sex just being sex. So Troy was all depressed and kind of laid low through the holidays, but he came back after Christmas with his driver's license and a new love: Monte. His Monte Carlo, that is.

Anyway, when I called the Meeting I was real clear that this was about the spring musical and NOT about sex. I wasn't saving myself for anyone in particular, but I wasn't planning on having sex just because I was turning 16 either. For one thing, if I ended up all depressed, I was pretty sure my parents weren't going to buy me a hot new car just to make me feel better. In fact, I already knew I wasn't getting a car until that summer.

Troy parked Monte in the back of the student parking lot. We all put on our hats and gloves and headed into school. "Any word on who's trying out for what parts?" I asked. I kicked a smooth gray stone up the sidewalk.

"You know Sarah Hensley will want the lead," Troy said, scooting the stone back my way.

"And Dustin Fairbanks," added Cassie. She intercepted the stone and kicked it 10 yards forward and off of a fire hydrant. CLANG! It disappeared in the dirty snow.

I nodded, scanning the sidewalk for another rock to kick. "Hamilton always gives seniors all the breaks."

"Well, there's no way Sarah can play Peter Pan," Troy said. "Her boobs'll get in the way."

"Definitely," Cassie agreed. "And Fairbanks' voice is too low. He looks like a grown man with a five-o'clock shadow. He's out."

"Yeah," I said. "You know he'll want to be the father and Captain Hook."

"Sarah will be Wendy," said Troy. "You can count on it."

"I guess that means Sandy will have to be Peter Pan," Cassie mused.

"What about Alex Parker?" I asked. "Hamilton might give the part to him since he's a junior. Or Katie Henry."

"I heard Katie's running track this spring," Troy offered.

"Alex's voice is changing," said Cassie. "I'm pretty sure he'd rather play baseball than sing."

I nodded. "I believe I've found my place. 'Second star to the right and straight on till morning.'"

Cassie and Troy looked at each other and rolled their eyes.

"What?" I said. "That's Peter Pan, not Shakespeare."

2

There was a star danced,
and under that was I born.

—*Much Ado About Nothing*, Act II, Scene i, Lines 349-350

I ALWAYS LOVED my *real* birthday when it finally arrived. It was my day, and I never wanted anything to ruin it.

On my last real birthday when I was 12, my mom scheduled a dentist appointment for me to get a filling. My parents said I was being overly dramatic, but I said what kind of a mom schedules pain on her child's birthday on purpose? Then Mom ended up stuck in court, so Dad had to take me. "Really, Sandy," he said, "don't you think you're over-reacting?"

"No thir," I said. My tongue was still numb. "Thith totally thuckth! Birthdayth aren't thuppothed to be painful!"

Dad laughed. "This is nothing compared to the pain your mom had 12 years ago on your birthday! Trust me, the older you get, the more painful birthdays become."

But my 16th birthday started out perfectly. Mom made my favorite "ABC" breakfast. "A" was for applesauce; "B" was for bacon; "C" was for cheese. She put a slice of American cheese on a piece of toast, topped that with four slices of crispy bacon and then smothered the whole thing in hot applesauce so that the cheese got all melty. Delicious! It was one of the benefits of being an only child. If my mom wanted to make my favorite breakfast for my birthday, then who was I to argue?

I swallowed and washed down my last bite with a gulp of cold milk. "Tryouts are after school."

Dad looked up from his newspaper at me. "Which part did you decide on?"

"Peter Pan, of course," I replied. I let out a crow and broke into my audition song. "I'm just the cleverest fellow 'twas ever my fortune to know." Mom clapped a couple times to encourage me, so I continued singing. "I taught a trick to my shadow to stick to the tip of my toe." Mom and Dad both jumped in at the end: "I gotta crow!" Dad dropped down to bass and Mom hit alto on the last note. They were smiling like they thought we might win an Emmy or something. I just laughed. My parents are so cheesy. If they think I'm overly dramatic, they should at least admit I get it from them.

Mom came over and gave me a big hug. "You'll do great!"

Dad nodded. "Break a leg."

"We'll celebrate your birthday and your audition at dinner tonight," added Mom.

"What time should I pick you up?" asked Dad.

"5:00 outside the auditorium," I replied.

We heard the loud roar of a motor and the thumping bass of a stereo in the driveway. "They're here. Gotta go!" I grabbed my coat and book bag and ran out the door.

I heard Dad call after me, "Wear your coat! Don't just carry it!"

I waved at him without looking back. *Like I would have frozen to death carrying my coat because I didn't know enough to put it on when I got cold.*

Cassie was in the front passenger seat, so I jumped in back. She turned down the stereo, and then she and Troy greeted me with our traditional birthday dirge.

"Happy birthday, happy birthday," they sang. "Pain and sorrow and despair, people dying everywhere, happy birthday, happy birthday." Their voices were meant for a dirge, and they sang it well.

"Thanks, guys!" I said.

"Better not give up your day job," Cassie said to Troy. "You can tune a car, but you need some help carrying a tune." Troy just laughed and turned the stereo back up. We jammed all the way to school.

As soon as Troy had parked and turned off the car, Cassie turned around in her seat to face me. "Are you nervous about try-outs?" she asked.

"Naaaah," I replied. "It's my birthday. I'm not going to waste the whole day stressing."

"Good for you," said Cassie.

Cassie and Troy exchanged a glance. Troy shrugged. I could tell they were thinking of last year when I was trying out for *Seussical.* I was totally freaking out all day.

I really wanted to be the Cat in the Hat, but so did Kristin Kennedy. She was a senior and used to getting whatever part she wanted-ed. She was so confident the part was hers for the asking that she didn't even bother to show up at the right time. I nailed the audition and got the part. Kristin ended up being Mazy the Lazy Bird. Just thinking about it still makes me smile.

"Maybe I am a little nervous," I told them, "but not like last year, if that's what you're thinking."

We climbed out of the car and headed into the school toward our lockers. As we went our separate ways, Troy slugged my arm. "You'll do great," he said with a grin. "Like always."

I nodded. "See you at lunch."

All morning I was thinking about tryouts. So much, that I almost forgot it was my birthday. I wasn't worried about singing the song or saying the lines or anything like that. But I found myself looking around at all the kids in this school wondering if anyone else really even cared about auditions. No one else wanted to go to Juilliard. In the whole history of West Side High School no one had ever even applied to Juilliard.

At lunch, Cassie and Troy got the West Side barbershop quartet to sing the real Happy Birthday song to me in four-part harmony and present me with a cupcake. Part of me felt embarrassed, but the whole key to acting is to free yourself from self-consciousness and fear. Sometimes I was still in the "fake-it-until-you-make-it" stage.

After lunch I started thinking about try-outs again. Last year after *Seussical* Hamilton told me he had never even considered giving such a major role to a freshman. "But you earned it," he said. He furrowed his brow and frowned like he was still trying to convince himself. Then he peered out at me over the rims of his glasses. "You've got talent." It sounded more like a curse than a compliment.

"I appreciate the opportunity," I said.

Hamilton just blinked at me, like he wasn't quite sure if I was mocking him. "Do you?" he inquired.

I nodded. "I know I can't sign up for drama class until I'm a junior, but I really want to go to Juilliard. The more experience I can get, the better."

Hamilton raised his eyebrows. "Juilliard?"

I nodded again. I think I was hoping he would get me into the drama class as a sophomore, but that didn't happen.

"You've got a long way to go to get to Juilliard," he replied. "That school attracts the most talented people in the world. And about 95% of *them* can't get in." He emphasized *them* as if I weren't one of them. "What makes you think they'll take you?"

I smiled with a confidence I did not actually feel. "I'm willing to work hard, and I've got you to teach me," I said.

Hamilton roared. He laughed so long and so hard that tears came to his eyes, and I started thinking about seeing if I could switch schools or maybe get Mom and Dad to homeschool me.

Finally, he took off his glasses and wiped his eyes on his corduroy jacket sleeve. "I'll tell you what, Sandy," he said. "If you work hard for the next three years—show up on time, every time, prepared—I'll do everything I possibly can, too."

I never told anybody about that conversation, but in the back of my mind, I really believed Hamilton would help me if he could. There were times, though, I wondered if Hamilton would actually remember his promise. Like for tryouts that day. If he does, and I show up prepared, the part should be mine.

That or something better, my mom's voice whispered in my head. Mom had this theory when things didn't go exactly her way that there was something even better out there that never occurred to her. It was all very optimistic and Zen, but I was more like Dad. I'd just as soon have what I wanted to begin with and not deal with the disappointment.

You get what you get, and don't throw a fit. That was what Cassie's mom always told us when one of us wanted what the other one got. God, I've got a lot of voices in my head. If I'm going to be Peter Pan in two hours, that's the voice I should be zeroing in on.

And so I did. "How clever I am!" I crowed uncertainly to myself. "Oh, the cleverness of me!" I'd need to convince myself first before I had any hope of convincing Hamilton.

3

Such tricks hath strong imagination
That if it would but apprehend some joy,
It comprehends some bringer of that joy;
Or in the night, imagining some fear,
How easy is a bush supposed a bear!

—*A Midsummer Night's Dream*, Act V, Scene i, Lines 18-20

EACH MINUTE OF the afternoon was like an empty boxcar on a slow-moving train to nowhere. I was ready to audition and be done with it.

I actually hate auditions. Sure there's the adrenaline and the vision in my mind of the perfect performance and the absolute knowing that I can do it, but it is really painful to watch other people totally crash and burn. At try-outs, everyone has to act all nice and proper, but you know the people competing against you for the part, plus all of their friends, are secretly hoping that you will screw up big time.

Once all of the parts were assigned, the cast would start to pull together as a team and really support each other. Hamilton really preached cooperation over competition once we all had our parts. I just needed to get through today.

13

I had study hall last period. This worked out great when we had plays and musical productions in full swing because I could get a pass from Hamilton and get a head start on rehearsals. Hamilton wasn't handing out passes today, though. So I signed out to go to the library in search of the real *Peter Pan*.

I went straight to fiction and started looking for the last name Barrie. I was pretty sure Mom and Dad had read *Peter Pan* to me when I was growing up, but I didn't really remember the book compared to the play or the movie versions. I came across a well-worn copy of the classic by J.M. Barrie and started flipping through the pages. Very near the end of the third chapter, these words jumped out at me: "I solemnly promise that it will all come out right in the end."

The words somehow reassured me. Of course, they weren't talking to me about my life. They were promising a "happily ever after" for Wendy and John and Michael Darling. Still, I wanted to believe these words for myself, too.

It was the kind of promise you'd never get from Shakespeare. Exactly the opposite. Shakespeare only guaranteed that things would NOT come out right in the end. He put it right in the title: *The Tragedy of Julius Caesar*, *The Tragedy of Macbeth*. *Hamlet, King Lear, Othello* … all tragedies. Talk about your truth in advertising. Everybody always dies in the end.

"It will all come out right in the end." Maybe if it doesn't seem right, it's not really the end. But right for who? My father's face appeared frowning before me in my mind. *For whom. It's the object of a preposition.* I had so many voices in my head, even then, before my own tragedy struck.

I checked out the book and found a seat at a table where I could read until the bell rang. Things I learned in those last few minutes before try-outs:

1. Barrie actually wrote the play first and the book seven years later. Like Shakespeare, Barrie was really a playwright.

2. The library clock was three minutes fast.

3. Barrie was a very short man and a very unhappy adult. He loved childhood and children, but never had any of his own. Children that is. I'm pretty sure he had a childhood.

4. Mrs. Randolph, the librarian, was way more disruptive hushing people than the people that she thought needed hushing.

5. The name Wendy didn't exist before *Peter Pan*. There was a little girl who tried to call Barrie "my friendy," but it always came out "Wendy."

Finally, the bell sounded. Students erupted into the hallway from every room. I resisted the flow toward the exits and began making my way to the auditorium.

"Hey, Sandy," a voice called from behind. "Wait up!"

I glanced backward and saw Shanika Washington. She played the Motown Bad Girl last year in *Seussical*. She was really good, too, and a senior this year. "Hi, Shanika," I called back. I held my ground as Shanika pushed her way toward me through the mass exodus. "Are you on your way to auditions?"

Shanika nodded. I turned to walk beside her. "Are you going for Peter Pan?" she asked.

"Definitely," I replied. We walked toward the auditorium together. "How about you? Which part do you want?" I held the door for her to walk in ahead of me.

"What part do I want or what part do I think I can get?" asked Shanika.

"What part do you want?" I asked again, this time with more emphasis on the want.

"Peter Pan, of course," she replied.

I laughed. "Peter Pan. Of course!"

Shanika tilted her head back and narrowed her eyes at me. "Are you dissin' me?"

I sobered quickly. "No way," I said. "The play's called *Peter Pan*, everybody who's anybody wants to be Peter Pan." To be honest, though, I'd never really pictured a black Peter Pan. In my mind, Peter could be a boy or Peter could be a girl dressed up like a boy, but who ever heard of a black Peter Pan?

We walked down the aisle together in silence. I found a seat toward the front of the auditorium and Shanika sat down next to me.

"I'd make a great Peter Pan," said Shanika. She nudged me with her elbow. "You should be worried."

I didn't know what to say. Voices bounced off the ceiling and the walls all around us, but I couldn't find mine.

"What?" Shanika shook her head. I couldn't tell if she was disgusted with me or amused by my embarrassment. "You don't think Peter Pan can be black?"

"Well, actually, I . . . I . . . " I just looked at Shanika.

"Shoot! And you think you can act?" Shanika was smiling now.

I threw my hands up and lowered my head. "I guess I've just never seen a black Peter Pan, and I never really thought about it. I'm sorry."

"You got nothing to be sorry about," Shanika said. "I'm the one who's sorry. I'm sorry your parents never read you *Amazing Grace*. That was my favorite book growing up."

"*Amazing Grace*?" I asked. "What's that about?"

"Not what—who," said Shanika. "It's about Grace, a little girl who loves stories." She leaned in toward me and drew out the word loves in a way that made me wonder if I ever loved stories as much as she did. "Grace loved stories so much that she acted every one of them out, and I acted them all out with her. Joan of Arc, Aladdin, Hiawatha, Mowgli… didn't matter what the story was, me and Grace, we always gave ourselves the most exciting parts."

Shanika leaned back in her seat. "Anyway, in the end, Grace got to be Peter Pan in the school play even though she was black and even though she was a girl."

"Sounds like a pretty good book," I said. I wished that auditions would hurry up and start already.

"So what was your favorite book when you were a kid?" Shanika asked.

My mind raced. *Why is she asking me this? Is she really going to try out for Peter Pan? Should I be worried?*

"Your mama and daddy did read to you, didn't they?" Shanika made it sound as if I must have had the most pathetic childhood ever.

"My parents read to me." My words had a defensive edge to them. I took a deep breath and remembered sitting on my dad's lap reading book after book. "My favorite was *Harold and the Purple Crayon.* Only my dad always read it *Sandy and the Purple Crayon.* He read me the story a hundred times before I realized that my name started with an 'S' and there wasn't a single 's' in 'Harold.'"

"I remember Harold." Shanika laughed. "That crazy bald kid who drew his own adventure." She stood up and stretched. Then she looked down at me just long enough to make me uncomfortable. "I like Harold," she said finally. "He had almost as much imagination as Grace." And with that she walked away.

17

I watched Shanika make her way through the crowd. She never did tell me what part she was really trying out for.

4

When you do dance, I wish you
A wave o' the sea, that you might ever do
Nothing but that, move still, still so,
And own no other function. Each your doing,
So singular in each particular
Crowns what you are doing in the present deeds,
That all your acts are queens.

—*The Winter's Tale*, Act IV, Scene iv, Lines 140-146

HAMILTON RAN AUDITIONS by classes rather than parts. He started with the seniors and worked his way down to the freshmen. He said it showed respect to the upperclassmen and was good "reality therapy" for the underclassmen. As a freshman last year trying out for the *Cat in the Hat*, I was one of the very last people to audition. Watching the upperclassmen go first actually helped calm me down and give me confidence. There were some people who were freaking out by the time it was their turn, though, and even some who just left and never tried out at all.

I went down to the front of the auditorium and signed in under sophomores. We had to give our first, second and third choices for the parts we wanted. I looked through the sign-up sheet and found

Shanika's name. Tiger Lily, Captain Hook and Peter Pan. I flipped back to my name and put down Peter Pan, Captain Hook and Wendy. Some dopey freshman named Gavin had written Peter Pan, Peter Pan and Peter Pan. I laughed. *No freshman is going to steal my part. Poor Gavin—you're destined to be a lost boy for sure.*

I made my way over to Mrs. Shields at the piano and told her that I would be singing, "I've Gotta Crow." Unlike the local youth theater where you never sang songs from the actual musical for auditions, Hamilton subscribed to the Broadway tradition. We each had to commit to a specific character and perform a song from Peter Pan. Mrs. Shields nodded and made a note to herself. Then I went back up to the very back of the auditorium and waited. It wasn't long before Hamilton called for order, gave us the instructions and wished us all good luck.

"All of the parts, including understudies, will be posted outside the auditorium on Monday morning," he said. "Do not call me or e-mail me or text me over the weekend. If you see me, you can smile and wave and say hello, but don't ask. In fact, you'd be better off not talking to me at all between now and then. If you can't wait to find out what part you got, you'll have no part at all."

He meant it, too. Last year Camden Reynolds' mom called Hamilton after auditions to tell him that Camden didn't test well, but would be perfect for the Horton the Elephant part. "I'm sure he would," Hamilton told his mom, "but too many directors spoil the play." At least that's Camden's story on how he ended up doing costumes and make-up.

I was singing quietly to myself along with the seniors trying out for main parts just to warm up my voice. Then Shanika came out. She took a flash drive to the sound guy and went to the center of the stage. Dressed all in black, she looked strong and confident.

She crossed her arms and nodded. The sound of beating war drums filled the auditorium. "I am Tiger Lily!" Shanika cried. And she began to dance.

She was good. Really good. Not only did she do cartwheels and all of the regular Tiger Lily moves, she added several back and front walkovers and two back handsprings followed by a back aerial. She even did the splits. "I am Tiger Lily!" she roared.

I felt sorry for every underclassman who signed up for Tiger Lily. How could anyone compete with that?

When the music stopped, there was a moment of silence as Shanika once again stood in the center of the stage with her arms crossed. Then the hushed auditorium exploded in thunderous applause. Arms still crossed, Shanika gave a formal bow before strolling back over to the sound guy to collect her flash drive.

Up until Shanika, I felt like I could do at least as well or better than every senior that auditioned, regardless of the part. *Maybe she's the one who should be applying to Juilliard.* I had enough rhythm that I could handle simple dance steps. With a little practice, I could probably do a decent cartwheel. But a back aerial? The splits? *Hey, you're applying to the Juilliard school of DRAMA, not dancing. Nobody expects you to dance like that.* My mom's lawyerly voice of reason. Great for her clients and the courtroom. Not much help when it came to tryouts.

Shanika slipped into the seat beside me. "What do you think?" she asked.

"I think you're amazing," I whispered.

Shanika beamed. "You got that right!"

"So where did you learn to do all that?" She wasn't a cheerleader. I didn't think she was on the school gymnastics team, either.

"Taekwondo," she replied. "You should see me with nun chucks."

"Do you break bricks with your forehead, too?" I asked. I slapped my palm on my forehead.

"Not bricks," she responded. "Just wooden boards, and only with my hands, feet and elbows." She extended her left hand, palm out, in front of her and cocked the heel of her right palm in by her side. Then pulling her left hand back in, she snapped her right palm forward with enough force to flatten me if I'd been in front of her instead of beside her.

I nodded. "Remind me never to pick a fight with you."

Shanika laughed and shook her head. "Sandy, I can't see you whoopin' anybody's butt anywhere but on a stage."

"You got that right," I agreed.

And with that, Shanika disappeared.

By the time it was my turn, the crowd in the auditorium had dwindled significantly. There was no applause from the audience and nothing but a nod from Hamilton, but I was pleased with my performance all the same. I was better than any of the seniors or juniors who tried out for Peter Pan. And I was the only one who sang, "I Gotta Crow." Everyone else did "I Won't Grow Up." *Attitude is everything.*

I thought about sticking around to watch Gavin-the-freshman crash and burn, but decided against it. I walked back to my locker and then down by the gym to see if Cassie was still there working out in the weight room. She was already showered, and it looked like the only thing holding her up was Aaron Jackson, the school's star wrestler. He had a full-ride scholarship to some Big Ten school in Michigan next year.

"Hey, Sandy." Cassie greeted me. "What's Shakin'? How'd the audition go?"

I gave her a thumbs up. "The world's mine oyster." I looked at Aaron, but he was totally ignoring me. He had his arm on the wall over Cassie's shoulder and looked like he was ready to pin her if I hadn't showed up.

Cassie nudged Aaron. "You know Sandy, right?"

"Right," Aaron grunted, but he still didn't look at me.

"My dad will be here at 5:00," I said to Cassie. "Want a ride home?"

"I'm her ride," Aaron snorted.

I gave Cassie a "what-the-heck" look, and she just shrugged.

"We'll pick you up around 6:30 then," I said. "We've got reservations at the Greek place for 7:00."

"Today's Sandy's birthday," Cassie explained to Aaron.

Aaron mumbled something that faintly resembled the words, "Happy Birthday, kid."

"Thanks," I said. "Thanks a lot." I waved to Cassie. Once again Aaron was totally ignoring me. I stuck my finger in my mouth making silent gagging motions.

Cassie giggled. "See ya, Sandy."

I waved to her again over the top of my head as I walked away.

5

Prepare for mirth, for mirth becomes a feast.

—*Pericles*, Act II, Scene iii, Line 7

WHEN WE ARRIVED at The Palace Athena, Troy was there waiting. Nikos, the owner, greeted me with a warm, European hug and kiss on the cheek and a lively "Happy Birthday, Sandy!" He shook hands with Dad, clapping him on the shoulder and nodded politely to Troy and Cassie. "Welcome," he said. Then Nikos reached for my mom's hand and raised it to his lips, planting a big ol' Greek kiss on her knuckles. "How's my favorite lawyer?" he asked.

Before he opened The Palace, Nikos was a used car salesman. He and some distant cousins in New York and Chicago were all indicted on federal fraud and conspiracy charges for rolling back the odometers on a bunch of vehicles. Mom represented Nikos, and the jury found him not guilty on all charges. Everyone else went to prison.

"You will sit at the best table!" he cried and led us toward the back wall with a huge mural of the goddess Athena standing in front of the Parthenon dressed like a warrior with an owl on her shoulder. Her face was the perfect reflection of my mother. When

Nikos said Mom was his favorite lawyer, he wasn't kidding. He pretty much worshipped the ground she walked on.

"Drinks on the house!" Nikos proclaimed as we each found a seat at the round table. "What can I bring you? Some Ouzo to start the festivities?"

Mom laughed and shook her head. "Soft drinks for the kids, Nikos. And I'll have an Alpha."

"Make mine a chardonnay," said Dad.

Nikos nodded and began handing out menus. "What soft drink for you, Sandy?"

"Club soda with lime, please," I said. Troy ordered a Mountain Dew and Cassie asked for a Cherry Coke.

"Very good," said Nikos. "I bring you pita and tzatziki to nibble. You need anything, anything at all, you just ask Nikos."

When a waitress returned with our drinks and appetizer, we took turns digging our triangular pita pieces into the yogurt and cucumber spread.

"No double dipping, Troy," Cassie announced.

"Man, I love this stuff," Troy replied through a huge mouthful. Cassie nodded, licking the corners of her mouth and reaching for more.

Dad ordered the Greek Feast for five, family style—plenty of kalamari, spanakopita, souvlaki and feta fries for everyone.

Next came the Greek salad. "Who doesn't want their banana peppers?" asked Cassie. She collected Dad's and mine, squeezed the stems off both and popped them directly in her mouth.

As we were finishing our salads and the last of the tzatziki, Mom pulled a brightly wrapped package from her purse and placed it on the table beside me. "Do you think there's time to open a gift now?" Mom asked, surveying the empty plates.

"Yeah," replied Cassie, "but can Sandy start with ours? Better save the best for last." She handed me what was obviously a DVD wrapped in shiny, red Happy Birthday paper.

"It's from both of us," Troy added.

"Thanks, guys," I said. I shook the package. Complete silence. "Should I try to guess?"

"Nah," replied Troy. "Just tear it open."

I lifted one taped end and let her rip. As the paper fell away I recognized the movie instantly. "The Blu-ray version of *Hamlet* with Kenneth Branagh and Kate Winslet! This is great!" I exclaimed. "Exactly what I wanted. Do you want to go back to my house after dinner and watch it?"

"No thanks!" Cassie and Troy nearly shouted in unison.

Mom and Dad laughed. "I thought you three were going out to see a movie afterwards," said Mom. She poured the last of her beer from the bottle into her glass.

"We are," said Cassie. She turned to me. "Maybe we'll get snowed in at your place before the winter's over and we can watch it together then."

"Right," I said.

A busboy began clearing our salad plates as the waitress filled the table with steaming meat kabobs, spinach pie and other succulent dishes. "Looks like we'll have to save our gift until dessert," said Mom. She passed the chicken souvlaki to me. "Your favorite. Happy Birthday, Sandy." Then she turned to a server. "Could we get more of the tzatziki, please?"

As we were passing the dishes and filling our plates, Nikos reappeared. "You like?"

"Everything's perfect as usual, Nikos," my father replied. He put all of his fingers and thumb together on his lips and made a soft kissing sound and released the kiss gently into the air. "Efharisto," he said. "Thank you very much."

"You are very welcome," Nikos replied. He put his hand on my shoulder. "Eat up, and then I bring you special dessert." True to his word, toward the end of the meal Nikos arrived with a large plate of Greek honey puffs. "Loukoumades!" he declared. The plate was covered with a mound of little pastries kind of like fried donut holes dipped in honey, rolled in cinnamon and sprinkled with walnuts. "Happy Birthday" was written around the edge of the plate in chocolate syrup and a cute little Greek flag flew proudly from the top puff.

All of the restaurant staff gathered round to sing "Happy Birthday" and added a loud "Opa!" at the end. As the staff cleared, a belly dancer slithered up to the table with little clanging finger cymbals, a beaded headdress, flowing scarves and lots of rings, bracelets and bangles. She danced with her palms together over her head and then with her palms out, shaking her hips so that all of her glittery fringe and tassels shimmered with her. Next she took me by the hand and pulled me up to do a belly dance with her. I followed her lead, throwing in a few shimmies of my own. I must have done a pretty good job, too, because everyone applauded. Then the whole restaurant roared with laughter when Nikos joined us.

Finally, it was time to eat the dessert and open my gift from Mom and Dad.

"A new iPhone!" I held the lime green gadget with everything anyone could ever want in my hands. "This is so cool," I whispered, turning it over and over again.

"Turn it on," Cassie urged. I pushed the button and the machine came to life.

"I'm so glad you like it," Mom said. She gave me a hug and kissed my forehead.

Dad nodded. "Happy Birthday, Sandy."

"I can't believe you got the new iPhone," Troy said. "We'll have to load it up with music and videos."

"Sounds good," I agreed.

Mom started gathering up the wrapping paper and trash, and Dad cleared his throat. *Uh, oh . . . I feel a lecture coming on.* But Dad didn't say a word. Instead, he pulled out his wallet and put three $50 bills in the middle of the table, side by side.

Troy and Cassie were staring, eyes wide open. "What's that for?" I finally asked.

"That little gizmo has apps and texting and internet and all kinds of capabilities," said Dad. "There have to be some rules that go along with it."

Mom smiled. "We thought maybe the three of you could help us come up with some reasonable guidelines . . . the cash is because we value your input."

"Just a little incentive," Dad added. "Each of you gets to suggest a rule, and if we all agree it's a good one, then you get $50. You go first, Sandy."

"Wow," I said. "Let me think." I took a deep breath. *Leave it to my parents to figure out a way to give me rules I can't complain about.* "I think no texting or surfing the internet in class would be a good rule." *Especially because that means I get to take the iPhone with me to school every day.*

Dad furrowed his brow and looked around the table. "Any discussion?"

Troy shrugged. Cassie nodded. Mom murmured, "Sounds like a pretty good rule to me."

Dad continued. "All in favor say 'aye.'" A resounding "aye" rang from the group. "Opposed?" Silence. He picked up the first $50 bill and handed it to me. "Okay. No texting or surfing the internet in class. Who's next?"

Troy jumped in. "I got one." I shot him a pleading look, but he was focused on the $50.

"Let's hear it, Troy," replied Dad.

"No texting, talking on the phone or surfing the internet while you're driving, Sandy." Troy looked at me and smiled. "I mean, it won't be long now before you have your license, right?"

"That's right," Mom chimed in. "I think that's an excellent rule. Any discussion?" She waited a moment and when no one said anything, she called for the vote, which was once again unanimous. She handed Troy a $50 bill. "This is going very well, don't you think, dear?"

Dad and I looked at each other. "Don't look at me," I joked. "You're 'dear.' I'm 'honey.'"

Dad grinned and turned to Mom. "It's going very well. Only, now poor Cassie has to go last. What do you think, Cassie? Can you come up with one more rule that we all can agree upon?" He reached for his glass of chardonnay and took a deep draw.

Cassie crossed her arms and pursed her lips, and I just knew she had something wicked in mind. Without missing a beat, she suggested, "How about no sexting?"

Dad spewed chardonnay clear across the table and grabbed for his napkin. Troy couldn't help snickering. Cassie just sat there cool as spring break in Alaska. Mom was the first to speak. "I agree completely. Absolutely no overexposed or under-clothed photos on the iPhone."

"Works for me," Troy piped up. He gave Cassie an approving nod. "No naked pics."

Dad didn't say a word. He just handed Cassie the last $50 bill and called for the check.

6

O, beware, my lord, of jealousy
It is the green-eyed monster which doth mock
The meat it feeds on.

—*Othello*, Act III, Scene iii, Lines 165-167

CASSIE, TROY AND I piled into Monte and headed to the movies. "I cannot believe you brought up sexting in front of Sandy's parents!" Troy said to Cassie once my parents were far behind.

"Hey," Cassie retorted, "50 bucks is 50 bucks. Plus, it's the perfect rule. You don't even want to sext, do you, Sandy?"

I shook my head. "Never even occurred to me."

"Well, you only had the iPhone for about a minute before Cassie came up with that rule," Troy countered. He held the steering wheel with his left hand nonchalantly and waved around his other hand holding up just his index finger.

Cassie reached up into the front seat and pushed on my shoulder. "Let me see the phone," she said.

I passed the phone back to her. "Still, it's a good rule," I admitted. "I don't see me ever wanting to break it."

"So what would you do if somebody sent you a picture like that?" Cassie asked.

I turned around in the front seat so I could see what she was doing. "Don't do it, Cassie," I warned.

"Do what?" Cassie responded. "I'm just checking out the music features."

"You can sext me, Cassie," said Troy. "That rule only applies to Sandy."

"In your dreams, dude." Cassie continued playing around with my phone. "I'm serious, Sandy. What would you do if somebody sexted you?"

"Nobody's going to sext me," I said motioning for her to give me my phone back.

"But what if somebody did?" Cassie persisted. "What would you do?"

"I'd delete it," I said very matter-of-factly. Then I switched to my "mom" voice. "Absolutely no overexposed or under-clothed photos on the iPhone." I motioned again for her to hand me the phone. "Why? What would you do?" I asked Cassie.

"I haven't decided yet," she replied mischievously.

Troy was eyeing Cassie in the rearview mirror. "Has that ape-man been sending you pictures of his banana?"

"His name is Aaron, and that's none of your business," Cassie retorted. "I was talking to Sandy."

Troy gripped the steering wheel tightly with both hands and gave a little huff. Whatever he wanted to say, he must have thought better of it.

"Look, Sandy," Cassie said flashing the phone back toward my face. "There's a song that's been downloaded already." She played around some more with the buttons. Suddenly Dolly Parton blared through my phone.

"Give me that!" I shouted.

Cassie laughed and tossed the phone back to me.

"What was that?" Troy asked.

"That would be my mom," I replied clicking the music off.

"It sure didn't sound like your mom," said Troy.

Cassie punched him on the shoulder and laughed. "It's not her singing. She downloaded a Dolly Parton song called 'To Sandy.'"

Troy and Cassie both went "awwwww" at the same time. Then Cassie said, "Isn't that sweet?" They laughed and all of the tension that had been building between them evaporated.

"What else did she put on there?" Troy asked.

"How should I know?" I groaned. "I just got it." I did a quick check through the music and photos, but didn't find any contraband or other potential embarrassments.

We found a place to park and each bought our own ticket to the show. "Anybody want popcorn?" Troy asked.

"Let's go find a good seat first," Cassie answered quickly.

As we walked down the hallway to the designated auditorium, I recognized Aaron leaning by the doorway, hands in his pockets.

"Hey, Cass," he said. He tried to plant a serious kiss on her lips, but she pulled away before he could even get his arms around her.

"What's he doing here?" Troy kind of thrust his chest forward and his shoulders back as he said it.

Aaron held up his ticket. "Free country," he grunted.

Cassie grabbed his other hand and led him into the theater. "Come on, you guys. Let's find some seats."

Troy and I followed. "He's got a lot of nerve just showing up here," Troy muttered under his breath.

"Cassie must have told him we would be here," I whispered back. "Maybe she invited him."

"Why would she do that?" Then more loudly he asserted, "It's your birthday."

Cassie ignored us and picked out four seats together in the center aisle. She made sure Aaron and Troy were on opposite ends. After we settled in, Cassie asked, "Anybody want some popcorn?"

Troy leaned back in his seat and crossed his arms. "I suddenly lost my appetite."

"I'm not hungry either," I said.

Cassie kind of bugged her eyes out at us, but drew them back in before she turned to Aaron. "Well, I am," she said in a syrupy voice. "Why don't you go get us some popcorn and sodas?"

"No problem," Aaron replied and made his way out of the row away from Troy and me.

As soon as he was gone, Troy leaned forward to get in Cassie's face. "What did you invite him for?"

"I didn't invite him," Cassie snapped. "I just told him I already had plans, and he showed up. What do you want me to do?"

Troy shook his head and bit his bottom lip. "Send him away before he ruins Sandy's birthday," Troy said. I detected something close to a tremble in his voice.

Cassie stood up and put her hand on her hips. "Aaron's not ruining Sandy's birthday. You are," she said pointing an accusing finger at Troy.

I put both of my arms up and out between them. "Guys! Enough!" I barked. "Nobody's ruining my birthday. My birthday's just fine. Let's just watch the movie, okay?"

Cassie glared at Troy, but finally sat back down. "Sorry, Sandy," she said.

"Whatever," Troy mumbled under his breath.

We sat in silence until Aaron returned. Fortunately, it was a really good movie. We all sat mesmerized for the next two hours. The only conflict was on the screen before us, and when that resolved, we felt like ourselves again.

The people all around us were leaving, but we stayed through the credits just listening to the music and feeling good. Finally, the lights came up, and we stood to go.

I leaned over toward Cassie and said, "When shall we three meet again?" I didn't want Aaron to hear me, but I did want Cassie to get the hint that she needed to ditch him and come with us. We needed to work out some kind of truce on the whole Ape-man issue, and that wasn't going to happen with Aaron around.

But Aaron took Cassie's hand, and she followed after him without saying a word to me. They were walking out in one direction, and Troy was leaving in the other. Part of me wanted to stay right where I was and make them all come back to me. But the ushers were already picking up trash and getting the place ready for the next show. I had to go, and it wasn't much of a choice. I hurried to catch up with Troy.

Cassie and Aaron were waiting for us by the main exit. He had his arm around her waist and his thumb stuck in her front pocket. Troy just looked away.

"So, Cassie," I said choosing my words carefully, "are we going back to my place?" Cassie knew that Aaron would not be invited without my parents' approval.

Cassie put her hand on the hand Aaron had latched to her pocket. "I don't know," she said. "Maybe we could all go back to my house. My mom won't care." But Cassie knew that Troy

35

wouldn't go anywhere if Aaron was going, too. So we all just stood there.

Finally, Troy nudged my arm with his elbow. "Come on, Sandy. I'll take you back to your house."

I nodded to Troy and then turned to Cassie. "Are you coming with us?"

She frowned and shook her head in Troy's direction. "Not right now," she said. "I'll catch up with you guys later."

Troy walked brusquely away without a word.

"Right. Later," I muttered before bolting off toward Troy.

We made our way through heavy traffic back to where Monte was parked. When we got there, Troy slammed both hands on the top of the car. "Man, I hate that guy!"

"Let's just go," I said. "Unlock the doors."

We got into the car, but Troy wasn't ready to let it go. "I really do hate that guy," he said again. "What does she see in him anyway?"

"Maybe he's got a big banana," I joked. Wrong thing to say. Troy didn't see the humor. "Look, I don't like him much either, but Cassie apparently does. And she's not going to listen to you because she thinks you're jealous."

"Jealous!" For a second I thought Troy was going to smack me. Instead, he turned the key and revved Monte a little harder than normal for such a cold engine. "How could I be jealous of someone I cannot stand?"

"I'm not saying you're jealous," I said. "I'm just saying Cassie might think you're jealous."

"Well, I'm not," Troy insisted.

"I know," I agreed. But I had a bad feeling about it all the same.

7

Beware the ides of March.

—*Julius Caesar*, Act I, Scene ii, Line 23

CASSIE DIDN'T CATCH up with us later that night or even the next day. She just sent Troy and me the same text: "Sorry. Don't be mad." They say March comes in like a lion. It wasn't snowing or anything, but it sure felt cold and ominous. Troy spent the weekend working on cars at his uncle's shop, and I spent the weekend loading music and hundreds of apps onto my new phone.

On Monday we all pretended like nothing was wrong. Hamilton posted the parts as promised. I got Peter Pan, and Shanika was Tiger Lily. We both showed up last period to get a jump start on rehearsals.

"I haven't seen you in study hall before," I said. "Who's letting you cut class to be here?" I started pawing through the packets of information and lines for each actor and pulled out ours.

Shanika shook her head as I handed her the Tiger Lily packet. "Not class. I just come to school in the mornings and work in the afternoons."

"And your boss is letting you off for the musical?" It seemed too good to be true. "Where do you work?"

"At my dad's taekwondo place."

"Must be nice," I replied. We started shuffling through our paperwork.

Shanika laughed. "I'm not complaining." She pulled out a Peter Pan-Tiger Lily duet. "Do you want to study our lines together or would you rather start with a song?"

"Let's start with a song."

The first two weeks of March passed quickly, but I could feel the lion still lurking. I spent less time with Troy and Cassie and lots of time rehearsing with Shanika. Finally, Cassie extended the olive branch and invited Troy and me to her house on Saturday afternoon. But we hadn't been there an hour before Aaron showed up. I thought Troy was just going to leave, but instead he decided to pull Monte into Cassie's garage and tinker under the hood.

"I just need to adjust the idle," he said. "Is it okay if I leave the garage door up so I don't accidently die of carbon monoxide poisoning?"

Aaron thought that was funny, and Cassie smacked him for laughing. "Definitely leave the door up," she said to Troy.

With Troy out in the garage, I was feeling pretty uncomfortable until Cassie asked me about the musical. It wasn't long, though, before I was talking more about Shanika than about Peter Pan. "Once the musical's over, I'm thinking about taking up taekwondo," I confessed. "New York's a big city. If I'm going to live there someday, it wouldn't hurt to know a little self-defense."

The words "self-defense" caught Aaron's attention. It was like he saw me for the first time. "Let me show you some wrestling moves for self-defense," he said. He started talking about posture and balance and take-downs and was totally showing off for Cassie. I wasn't impressed, but at least we were both making an effort to get along for Cassie's sake. Or so I thought.

I can't remember now if Aaron sent Cassie out into the kitchen to get us something to drink or if she went out on her own, but as soon as she walked out of the room, Aaron pinned me.

He looked me straight in the eyes. "Try to get up."

I struggled, but I couldn't break free from his hold. Aaron-the-ape-man was on top of me and wasn't about to let me up. He reeked of Axe cologne. His hot breath wrapped itself around my neck and sent a chill down my spine. I couldn't breathe, and was just about to say so when he put his hand over my mouth. All of a sudden I realized I could feel his big "banana" on my thigh like the big, bad wolf beating on my door, shouting, "Let me in!"

My heart pumped furiously, and my eyes began filling with tears. I thrashed around trying to fight him off, but he was too strong. I couldn't get him off me. I could feel myself starting to panic. I stopped struggling and just tried to breathe. Cassie was right there. Nothing was going to happen.

But I was wrong again. Aaron shoved his hand down the back of my pants, and I felt his fat middle finger go into my butt. If Cassie hadn't been there he might have just torn my pants right off. At that moment I didn't know what he was capable of. I tried to scream, but it came out more like a muffled growl. I was trying to bite his hand and squirm away when we heard Cassie coming back. Aaron jumped off me. As soon as his hand came off my mouth, I heard myself yell.

"What's all the commotion about?" Cassie asked. She set down a tray of drinks and snacks on the coffee table. I lay on the floor trembling.

"Sandy put some pretty good moves on me," Aaron lied. "I guess my training just kicked in, and I went straight for the pin."

Cassie walked over and gave him a hug. "All that weight-lifting—you don't know your own strength!"

Aaron held up his index finger all proud and erect. "I'm still number one." Then he laughed and turned to me. "I guess you'll have to settle for number two." He was holding up two fingers then, and I knew the second one was the middle finger he'd just stuck inside me.

Cassie started laughing, too. I tried to stand up, but my head was pounding and my ears were ringing. Aaron grabbed me and yanked me to my feet. "I must have knocked the wind out of you," he said. "Sorry."

I couldn't breathe, let alone speak.

"No hard feelings?" Aaron said.

I looked at Cassie. She was totally buying his act. "I need some fresh air," I said shakily. I grabbed my coat and walked out to the garage.

Troy peeked out from under Monte's hood. He took one look at me and came around to where I was standing. He was still holding a screwdriver in his hand. It had such a startling effect on me. I stifled a scream and felt myself backing away. "Are you okay?" Troy asked.

I shook my head.

"Want me to take you home?"

I shook my head again. My heart was pounding in my throat, making it impossible to breathe. I swallowed hard. I tried to imagine telling him. What would he do? I envisioned Troy going in there and attacking Aaron with the screwdriver. Cassie crying. Blood everywhere. I imagined Aaron wrestling the screwdriver away from Troy and stabbing him. I shuddered. "I just need some fresh air," I said. And I started walking.

I don't know where I thought I was going. I was just trying to get away. Away from there. Away from Aaron. Away from what had just happened. Away from what might still happen. Away. When I realized I was walking directly into the wind, I zipped up my coat, pulled up the hood and thrust my hands in my pockets. *Just keep walking.*

I must have walked for a long time, because next thing I knew I was several miles out of town, down by the river. There was an old covered bridge off to my right that crossed over the river into a state park. We used to love to play there when we were kids. The river wound around for several miles and then came back to only about a quarter mile south of here. In the summertime, people rented big inner tubes and floated off down the river. They'd float for two or three hours, depending on how high and fast the current was, until they came to the place to catch a shuttle back to the state park.

I wanted to jump in the river and float away. Nearly all of the winter's snow had melted so the waters were moving quite rapidly. The only bits of snow left along the banks were dirty, black and ugly. I stood at the edge of the covered bridge and wondered where I could possibly go from here. I felt like if I crossed that bridge, I would never come back. *Who am I kidding? There is no bridge that will take me away and none that leads back to where I was.* I sat down at the edge of the river and cried.

8

"Aaron, I see thou wilt not trust the air with secrets."

—*The Tragedy of Titus Andronicus*, Act IV, Scene ii, Line 169

I WAS STILL sitting at the bank of the river when I heard my phone
go off. It was a text message from Cassie.

"Where r u?"

I replied, "@ river"

"Howd u get there?"

"Walked"

"R u ok?"

"Yes"

"Where @ river?"

"Park bridge"

"Stay where u r. We'll come get u"

And so I stayed. Of course, when Cassie said "we'll come get
you" I thought she meant she and Troy were coming. I had it all
worked out in my mind that I would just tell them. I wouldn't say a
word until they asked me what was wrong, and then I would just
blurt it out. Just say it. *Say what? Aaron raped me? Only that's not really
it. Aaron stuck his finger in my butt?* It sounded almost absurd, even to

me. *Aaron sexually assaulted me? That's it. That's what he did.* But still that seemed pretty unbelievable. Aaron was popular. Aaron had Cassie. Why would Aaron mess with me?

"I don't know!" I screamed for the whole world to hear. My voice echoed back at me, a mocking whisper in my mind. *I don't know. I really don't know. Aaron will deny it. He'll laugh in my face. But Cassie and Troy are my best friends. They'll believe me. They have to believe me. I'll just say it.*

I heard a car pulling up to the bridge. I gathered all of my courage and determination and stood up. But when I turned to face my friends, I saw a black Ford Mustang. I held my breath hoping Troy and Monte would pull up behind them, but no luck. It was Cassie and Aaron.

I felt a jolt, and then my body started trembling all over. *Oh, my God! Cassie expects me to get in Aaron's car.* I honestly thought I was going to throw up. If I could have moved, I would have run all the way home and locked the door behind me. But I really couldn't move. Aaron stepped out of the Mustang and leaned back against the driver's-side door, arms crossed and lips curled up in a truly sinister grin. Cassie jumped out of the passenger-side door and ran down to meet me. She saw me trembling and pulled me up toward the car.

"You're freezing!" she exclaimed. "Get in the car where it's warm."

And the next thing I knew I was trapped in the back seat of Aaron's beastly car. And I wasn't about to say a word. Aaron was pretending to be all concerned—pretending like he didn't do anything—and that's what I was supposed to do, too. I tucked my hands in under my armpits and closed my eyes. My mind was racing to keep up with my heart. Just when I thought my head would explode, it came to me. *That's it. I'm supposed to act like nothing happened. No problem. If there's one thing I can do and do well, it's act. I'll just act like nothing happened. For now.*

"Turn up the heat," Cassie ordered.

Aaron complied. Then he started digging around underneath his seat. "Try this," he said, handing a bottle to Cassie who was sitting in the front passenger seat.

Cassie shook her head. "I told you, Sandy and Troy don't drink."

"No, you told me Sandy and Troy don't party." Aaron threw the car into reverse. Gravel flew as we spun around and sped away. "Just pass the bottle back to Sandy."

Cassie stared at me blankly until I nodded. She handed me a bottle of peppermint schnapps.

"Are you sure?" She watched me quizzically.

I unscrewed the cap and braced myself. *Do it just like a shot of Nyquil.* I took a deep breath and held the air in my lungs before taking two big gulps from the bottle. It burned all the way down my throat and into my stomach, but as I exhaled I felt a warming, tingling calm start to radiate out through my body.

I could feel Aaron watching me in his rearview mirror. I took two more quick gulps before handing the bottle back up to Cassie.

"All righty, then," she said. She tossed her head back and took a swallow.

"Send it this way," Aaron said, reaching his right arm out toward the bottle.

"Not while you're driving, Aaron," answered Cassie.

He tickled her side. "Aw, come on. I'm cold, too."

Cassie laughed and slapped his hand away playfully. "You get Sandy home safely, and then I'll be happy to warm you up."

Aaron laughed and put both hands back on the steering wheel. He was still watching me in the rearview mirror. "Oooh, baby! I like the sound of that," he said.

I could feel the tears starting up again behind my eyes. I sniffled and wiped my face on my coat sleeve. Then I motioned for Cassie to hand me the bottle again. Two more big gulps kept me acting like nothing had happened all the way home.

By the time the Mustang pulled into my driveway, it was dark out.

"Seriously, Sandy, are you going to be okay?" Cassie asked.

"I'll be fine," I said. "Thanks for the ride home."

"You're welcome," Aaron cut in, like he actually believed I was talking to him.

My heart rapid-fired like a submachine gun spitting out beats like bullets as Cassie slowly opened the passenger-side door, climbed out and put the seat forward for me. I could barely breathe, but I leaped out of the car as soon as the path was clear.

"Hold on," Cassie said to Aaron and then slammed the car door shut behind her. "Sandy, what's going on?"

A cold wind had us both bundling ourselves up and made it easy to avoid any real explanation.

"Nothing," I said. "I'm fine."

Cassie opened the car door. Before she ducked back inside she said, "Call me later."

I nodded.

"Promise?"

I nodded again. "Later," I said.

My parents were at some business dinner with one of Mom's clients, so I had the house to myself. That was lucky for me. I'm not sure how I would have dealt with my parents. They would have known something was up and probably would have figured out that I'd been drinking, too. My parents could be cool, but they definitely would not be cool with underage drinking.

I went into the kitchen and found a note from Mom. They would be back late, and there was a casserole in the refrigerator I could reheat if I hadn't eaten with Troy and Cassie. I opened the refrigerator. I saw the casserole, but I really wasn't hungry. There was an unopened jug of chardonnay on the top shelf by the milk and a half bottle of red wine with the cork stuck back in it. Mom always put the red wine on top of the refrigerator, but Dad always put it inside the fridge. It was an ongoing battle and the only thing they seemed to genuinely disagree on.

I pulled out the open bottle, removed the cork and poured a little in a juice glass. I'd tasted wine and beer in Mexico last year. My parents didn't mind because it was legal there, but I didn't really like the way it tasted, so I didn't actually drink much—just a taste of whatever Mom and Dad ordered.

I smelled the red wine in the juice glass and wrinkled my nose. Then I just downed it. It made the sides of my tongue tingle like a sweet tart, but there was no sweet, only tart. I put the cork back in the bottle just like it was before and stuck the bottle back in the refrigerator.

I rinsed out the juice glass and wandered into the formal dining room where my parents kept a cabinet full of liquor. Way in the back I found an old bottle of peppermint schnapps. No telling how long it had been there. I'd never seen my parents drink it. It was probably older than I was. I turned the bottle around and examined the label. There was no expiration date so I unscrewed the lid and poured about an ounce into the juice glass.

It smelled just like the stuff I had earlier, so I drank it. It tasted just like the other stuff, so I poured some more in the glass and took a big drink. It felt like a cleansing fire. Totally relaxing as soon as the burning passed. It looked like water. *Fire water.* I laughed and poured myself another glass. By the time I finished the bottle, I was feeling pretty good.

I decided to refill the empty bottle with water and put it back in the back of the cabinet where I'd found it. I'd be old enough to buy some real schnapps to refill it in five years, and my parents would probably never know. It seemed like the perfect plan, only while I was in the kitchen trying to refill the bottle, I got it too full, and while I was pouring water back out of it and checking to see how full it still was, I accidentally dropped it, and it shattered all over the kitchen floor.

Normally, I'd be upset that I had a mess to clean up, but the broken bottle actually cracked me up. I couldn't stop laughing. It was like when I was full of water, I was breakable, but now that I was out of tears and full of schnapps, I was shatterproof, and the bottle filled with water, well, of course, it had to break in my place.

It was quite a production cleaning it all up, though—the mop, the broom, lots of paper towel and—oh sorry—no recycling this glass and paper. I wrapped all of the broken glass and wet paper towel in a brown paper grocery bag and tied that up in a plastic grocery sack, and hid that in the big garbage can out in the garage.

There. Just like it never happened.

I went to my room and flung myself down on the bed. *Bam! Shatterproof!* I closed my eyes and laughed like a maniac. When I opened my eyes, the room was spinning. I closed my eyes again, but there was no stopping the spinning. I started to feel so dizzy and nauseated; I knew I was going to throw up. I tried to stand up to walk to the bathroom, but the spinning only got worse. I fell back down to my knees and crawled to the toilet where I threw up. And I just kept throwing up. Even when there wasn't anything left inside me to throw up, I still kept throwing up. I flushed my guts down the toilet. *Nothing left but the empty, shatterproof bottle.*

I needed a shower, but the idea of standing up for very long seemed impossible, so I filled the bathtub with hot water. *Only hot, no cold. Scalding hot. Fire water.* I struggled into the tub and submerged myself in the boiling water to sterilize myself. It burned, but it felt good. I let myself sink all the way down until the water covered my mouth and the steam filled my nostrils. As the hot water relaxed the knots in my stomach and released the tension in all of my muscles, I felt like I might fall asleep. *To be or not to be. Just go to sleep. To dream… or not. Off to Neverland. Never-again-land. Let your body slip down a couple more inches and never wake up . . . Maybe I will.*

9

"It is a tale
Told by an idiot, full of sound and fury,
Signifying nothing."

—*Macbeth*, Act V, Scene v, Lines 26-28

I AWOKE WITH a start. The water had cooled almost to the point of chilling me. When I tried to stand, my head pounded and my eyes burned. I sat back down and splashed the cool water on my face. *Just get yourself dried off and back to bed before Mom and Dad get home.* It seemed like a simple enough plan, but it was all I could do to roll myself over the side of the tub and out onto the bathmat. My head pounded relentlessly as I dried myself off, pulled on a pair of sweats, and finally escaped into my bed.

I felt my mom's hand on my forehead, then on my cheeks. "No fever."

I rubbed my eyes and tried to sit up. A sledgehammer smacked me right between the eyes. I winced and fell back. "I don't feel very well," I mumbled.

"I guess not," Dad said. "It's almost noon."

"Maybe it was something I ate." *Or drank. Let's not go there.*

"Are you sick to your stomach?" Mom asked. "What did you eat?"

"Last night? I don't know. Stuff at Cassie's."

"How do you feel now?" Mom asked.

"My head hurts. My stomach hurts. I just want to sleep."

Mom nodded. "Let's get you some Tylenol for the headache and some ginger ale to hydrate you and settle your stomach."

"Sounds good," I said. So I took my Tylenol and several sips of ginger ale and went back to sleep.

The next time I woke up, I felt a little better. My head had stopped pounding, and I just felt really thirsty. I chugged the glass of ginger ale, then made my way to the bathroom. I held my thoughts until I was once again safe in bed. Then it all came back to me. Aaron. Walking. Aaron's car. Drinking. Shattered glass. I rolled over and buried my face in my pillow. After a while I turned over again, but I somehow felt more suffocated with my face out of the pillow. I stayed on my back, and put the pillow over my face. That seemed to be just the right amount of suffocation for me to start to think clearly.

I had promised to call Cassie. If I didn't call her, she'd know something was really wrong. *If I call her now, I can just tell her I got sick last night. I'm still not feeling well today. I'll see her tomorrow at school. Short. Sweet. Just enough to get by. Texting would be even easier.* I got my phone and sent the message.

Only Cassie didn't text me back. She called me. Immediately. If I didn't answer, she'd know I was blowing her off. So I answered. "Hey."

"Hey, yourself. Are you okay?"

"I threw up last night, but I feel better today. I just want to sleep."

"You threw up?" I could almost hear her mind calculating how much I drank from the bottle of schnapps she handed me—which wasn't much compared to the bottle I drained at home.

"It wasn't that," I said hoping to reassure her.

"I know," she said.

I felt myself panicking. "What do you mean you know?"

"I mean Aaron told me what happened."

No. No way. No words came.

"And Aaron wanted me to tell you he's sorry."

Aaron's sorry? Just like that? He sexually assaults me and tells his girlfriend who's supposed to be one of my best friends in the world, and he's sorry and what? I'm supposed to say it's okay, no problem, let's just all be friends? This isn't making any sense.

"Sandy? Are you there?"

I think I liked it better when we were pretending nothing happened. "I'm here."

"It was all a big mistake. When the two of you were wrestling on the floor, Aaron said he all of a sudden thought you were coming on to him and it freaked him out, so he just pinned you, really hard and really fast."

I struggled to find my voice first and then to form the words: "He thought I was coming on to him?"

"I told him that was crazy—you're not like that. Anyway, he's sorry if he hurt you or scared you. He didn't mean it."

I came on to him. My fault. His mistake. He's sorry. He didn't mean it. I tried to wrap my mind around what she was saying, what Aaron had told her. What I was supposed to say? There was nothing I could say.

"Sandy?"

"Yeah?"

51

"Say something."

"What do you want me to say?" Anger spontaneously combusted in every cell of my being.

"Look, I know you and Troy don't like Aaron. I'm not asking you to like him. Just don't be mad, okay?"

"Don't be mad?" I knew I'd better choose my words carefully. "He … assaults me, and you want me to say I'm not mad?"

"He didn't assault you!" Cassie's frustration was becoming evident. "Maybe he insulted you. But at least he didn't mean to, and he said he's sorry. What more do you want? A personal, written apology?"

"I don't know what I want," I said finally. There was a long pause. I wanted to tell her what really happened and what a snake Aaron was, but somehow I knew she wasn't going to believe me. Her words were still ringing in my ears: *He didn't assault you!*

"So what am I supposed to do?" she asked.

I felt myself losing Cassie. Not just in this conversation, but really losing her. "Just let me go back to sleep."

"Fine. You go back to sleep."

"Bye."

I could hear her saying, "I hope you feel better . . . " as I hung up the phone.

I did not feel better. In fact, I felt decidedly worse with no hope of ever feeling better again. So much for pretending nothing happened. My whole life was suddenly swirling around in the toilet bowl. All that was left was the *glug, glug, glug* of being washed down the drain and into the sewer forever.

Aaron might as well have cut out my tongue and cut off my hands. *Shakespeare.* I pulled out *Shakespeare: The Complete Works* and started reading *The Rape of Lucrece.* I was thinking it was a play, but it was a poem, based on a Roman legend. I skimmed through the 22-page poem looking for the part where the rapist cut out his victim's tongue and cut off her hands so that she could never tell or even write about what had happened to her. It wasn't there. Instead, Lucrece tells her husband General Collatine what happened, makes his armies promise to avenge her honor, and then stabs herself in the heart.

I flipped back to the beginning and read the poem all the way through. The rapist was Tarquin. He was the son of the Roman king and a good friend of Collatine's. It's all about Tarquin's lust and Lucrece's beauty and honor. In the end, though, there's no real revenge. Lucrece is dead, Tarquin is only banished, and Collatine seems more upset by the loss of his rapist friend than the violation, torture and death of his wife.

That wasn't what I was expecting. I felt so confused by everything. One thing for sure: This was definitely a bad omen. Cassie would choose Aaron over me. She already had. Troy hated Aaron, but in the end, he would choose Cassie over me. There was a sense of finality in the realization. *It's a done deal. No matter what I do, I'm bound to lose.* I closed the book.

One line from the poem stayed with me, though, haunting me—taunting me: "Then where is truth, if there be no self-trust?" *Where is the truth? Can I even trust myself?*

I lay back down on the bed. Never in my life had I felt so lost and all alone. I wasn't just empty. It felt like I'd swallowed a black hole that was gradually sucking me into its cold, dark nothingness.

As I lay there, the only thing I could think about was having another drink. Not peppermint schnapps and not as much as I'd had last night, but just the right amount. A comfortable amount—somewhere between relaxed and numb, but nowhere near the head-spinning, gut-wrenching drunkenness. I needed to learn to pace myself better.

I started thinking about all of the bottles in my parents' liquor cabinet. Which ones were oldest, which ones were farthest toward the back, which ones were clear like water. Two came to mind. One was a bottle of rum that was at least as old as that bottle of schnapps had been. The other was peppered vodka that my dad had bought for Bloody Mary's that neither one of them particularly liked.

Both looked enough like water that I could empty them into water bottles and stash them in my room. Then I could refill the real bottles with water for now. *Just a couple of bottles, just to give me some time to sort everything out and find a way through this.*

10

Oh, unseen shame! Invisible disgrace!
Oh, unfelt sore! Crest-wounding, private scar!

—*The Rape of Lucrece*, Lines 827-828

"HEY, SANDY," TROY said as I climbed into the car Monday morning. "What's shakin'?"

"Now is the winter of our discontent," I replied, quoting the first line of *Richard III*. I positioned my backpack between my feet on the floor in front of my seat.

"Yeah, well, only three more days 'til spring." Troy pulled out of my drive and onto the street. "And only three more weeks until spring break!"

I nodded. "Where's Cassie?"

"With Aaron, I guess," said Troy.

I nodded again. I didn't trust myself to say anything, so I just stared out the window.

"Did you guys have a fight or something?" Troy was trying to look cool, but I could tell he was feeling pretty uncomfortable by the way he gripped the steering wheel and avoided looking my way.

"No," I replied. "When have the three of us ever fought?"

"I don't know. It's just she's acting all weird, and you're all 'winter' and 'discontent.' I'm just trying to figure out what's going on."

I tried to let out a normal, even sigh, but I could feel my insides trembling. I sucked in as much air as my lungs could hold and tried again to release it steadily. Then I said, "Well, if you figure it out, you let me know, okay?

"Right."

He turned up the stereo, and we didn't say anything else all the way to school. I had taken a shot of the vodka just before I left home and had some more in a water bottle in my backpack. I was really tempted to take another swallow right there in the car with Troy just to calm my nerves, but I wasn't sure whether he would be able to smell the pepper in it or even if I could take a swig and make it look like it was only water.

Fire water. Guaranteed to burn the pain away. Disinfect me. Keep me sterile. Sterile? Not that kind of sterile . . . okay, maybe that kind of sterile, too.

I admit that I did take a little "shot of courage" over the lunch hour to get me through the afternoon. Then I could stop being Sandy and start being Peter Pan.

Shanika and I were supposed to be rehearsing together, working on the part where Peter Pan says if he ever gets in trouble, he'll just send for Tiger Lily, and Tiger Lily says she'll just send for Peter Pan. I started wondering if maybe Shanika might be willing to help me. She's a senior and probably knew people over 21 who might buy alcohol for us if we paid them.

So maybe I seemed more distracted than usual. Maybe I was fixating just a little about where to get some more alcohol because that bottle I brought with me this morning was disappearing too fast, and I couldn't keep raiding my parents' liquor cabinet or I'd get caught. But it's not like I NEEDED the alcohol, not really. I wasn't addicted or anything. It was just for security purposes. I'd feel better knowing it was there. Just in case. *Just in case what?*

"Yo, Peter Pan!" Shanika snapped her fingers at me. "What is up with you today?"

"Nothing. I'm fine."

"Why don't I believe you?"

"I give up." I threw my hands up in the air for dramatic effect. "Why don't you believe me?"

"Are you kidding?" She thumped one of the hand drums she was holding. "Pay attention or I'll stop beating this drum and come beat your sorry little butt. You're making me look bad."

I pushed everything out of my head except Peter Pan and let myself be totally present in Neverland.

After rehearsal, instead of calling Dad right away to come pick me up, I walked out with Shanika. "I'm really sorry I was so out of it today."

"We all have good days and bad days. It's just the first time I ever saw you have a bad day on stage, you know?" Shanika sat down on a bench in the hallway to change from shoes to flip-flops for taekwondo. "But you came around." She laughed. "And I didn't even have to beat your butt!"

I nodded.

"I will if I have to, and you better know it!" Shanika raised her eyebrows at me and threw in a little head bobbing for effect.

I realized there was no way I was going to work up the courage to ask her to buy alcohol for me. Not today, anyway. "Maybe I ought to follow you to taekwondo just so I can learn a few tricks to defend myself."

"You can if you want. I'll be teaching a white belt class, so you could try it out of you're interested."

"Do you really think right in the middle of the spring musical is a good time for me to take up a new hobby?" I asked.

Shanika laughed. "Up to you, Sandy. Taekwondo relaxes me. At the same time it keeps me feeling strong and focused." She pulled out her car keys and stood up. "Are you going anywhere spring break?"

I shook my head and followed her out of the building.

"You could do the rank-advancement camp that week and go right from white belt to yellow belt just like that." She snapped her fingers. She talked some more about the different belts and what they mean. When we got to her car, she asked, "So are you going with me, or what?"

I wanted to. Actually, I just wanted to stand there in the parking lot talking to Shanika forever, but she had to go. And I wasn't sure I could keep it together long enough to go with her that evening. I really wanted to go home, have a drink, and think this all through.

"Not tonight," I said. "But I'll think about it. Especially the spring break thing."

"Up to you," Shanika said again as she climbed in the driver's side. She closed the door, rolled down the window and waved. "See you tomorrow!" she called as she drove away.

I called Dad to come get me as I walked back up to the building. Then I went into the restroom, checked under all the stall doors and when I was absolutely certain there was no one else around, I pulled out the vodka I had left in my water bottle. I stood in front of the mirror and tried to drink it down smoothly like water. I got it down, okay, but I couldn't keep my eyes from watering. *I need more practice. Or maybe I'll have to cry out the rest of these tears. Not here, though. Not now.*

I splashed cold water in my face and stood over the sink until the water stopped dripping. Then I looked at myself in the mirror. Only it wasn't me that I saw staring back with empty eyes. It was some walking zombie. I reached for a paper towel.

I look in the mirror.
Don't like what I see.
I don't want to face this reflection of me.
The frustration is there. All the loneliness, too.
I can't hide it from me.
Can I hide it from you?

Dad would be outside any minute. What would he see? What would I say? I pulled a stick of spearmint gum from my backpack and chewed it slowly as I walked out of the building.

"Feeling better?" Dad asked when I slid into the car.

I nodded. "I'm just tired."

"Are you hungry?"

I shook my head. "Not very. I just want to take a hot shower and crash."

"Probably not a bad idea," said Dad. "School okay today?"

I nodded.

"Rehearsal go okay?"

I nodded again.

"Let's just get you home."

When we got home, Mom made sure I didn't have a fever (I didn't), and then fed me some white rice and ginger ale before sending me up to shower and go to bed.

I lay awake until after I heard my parents go to bed. I picked up my phone. No texts from Troy or Cassie. I thought about texting them. I could call a Meeting of the Minds. Get this whole Aaron thing cleared up once and for all. But I couldn't quite shake Cassie's words. *He didn't assault you!* She had a point. Where were my bruises? It all happened so fast. *No blood, no foul. Get over it.* Even if Cassie wouldn't believe me, I could still tell Troy. He hated Aaron. He'd believe me. I could tell Troy.

But not tonight. Maybe in the morning . . . on the way to school. . .if Cassie isn't there. Or maybe not. Maybe if I take a drink first, for courage. I got up and pulled out the rum-filled water bottle. I opened the cap and tried to take a drink the way you would from a real water bottle. I felt my body jerk as I swallowed and kept my mouth shut tight to make sure the rum stayed down. When I finally breathed in, my nostrils were full of pungent, sweet fumes. I took one more swallow. I did much better on the second one.

That's enough. You have to pace yourself. It wasn't until I lay back down in my bed that the tears filled my eyes. They rolled down the sides of my cheeks toward the middle of my ears, but then skirted down around my earlobes and onto my neck before dropping onto my pillow. My nose filled completely up until I had to open my mouth to breathe. I opened my mouth reluctantly, uncertain what sound might escape.

It was the roar of the ocean—not like when you're standing right there as the waves crash on the beach, but like when you're somewhere far away and put a conch shell to your ear. I could cry all night long, but my tears would never drain the ocean dry. High tide. Low tide. High tide. The tears would come and go. Ebb and flow. No matter how hard I cried, they would never really be gone.

11

Diseases desperate grown
By desperate appliance are relieved,
Or not at all.

—*Hamlet*, Act IV, Scene iii, Lines 9-11

I NEVER INTENDED to steal anything. When I walked into the grocery store the next Saturday, I just wanted to see how much a bottle of vodka would cost. I needed to know so when I worked up the courage to ask someone to buy it for me, I'd know what to expect. There was no one watching. I reached out and picked it up. I walked away from the liquor aisle in search of a less conspicuous place to inspect the bottle more closely. But then I was afraid someone would see me carrying the bottle, so I slipped it into my backpack.

I really was going to put it back. I walked around the store for several minutes looking for an opportunity, but it was just too risky. I went to the candy aisle and selected a multi-pack of gum. I held my breath as I paid for the gum and felt a surge of adrenaline when I walked out of the store. I just kept walking, never looking back. It was way too easy. So I tried another grocery store several days later. Then another. I didn't like taking the bottles without paying for them. I wanted to pay for them so it wouldn't be stealing, but that wasn't an option. At least not until I found someone I could trust to buy a bottle for me.

I always bought something while I was in the store. In fact, I started buying Nyquil because it had quite a bit of alcohol in it. But it was loaded with other stuff, too, so I wasn't sure how much I could drink without accidently overdosing on it. Vodka felt so much safer and more effective.

I totally avoided Cassie and Aaron. Aside from Troy and Shanika, nobody at school seemed to notice anything. My parents knew something was up, though. Mom checked my temperature daily, and Dad kept asking me if I was hungry. Finally, the week before spring break they sat me down in the living room and asked me what was going on.

"We're really worried about you, Sandy," Mom said. "You just haven't been yourself since you had that bout with the flu two weeks ago."

I felt my throat tighten as panic shot from my stomach out through my fingers and down to my toes. I shrugged my shoulders and swallowed hard. "I'm just feeling tired, that's all."

"But you go to bed early every night," Dad said. "And you're sleeping in later, too."

"And you still don't seem to have your appetite back," Mom said. "I keep thinking you might have mono, but you haven't had a fever at all."

Dad looked at me earnestly. "What do you think it is that's making you so tired all the time?"

"I don't know." I barely whispered the lie.

Mom and Dad looked at each other. Dad shook his head; then Mom came and sat beside me on the sofa. She kissed my forehead. "Still no fever," she reported. "But there's something going on in there."

Dad nodded. "Is there something that's upsetting you? We haven't seen much of Troy or Cassie the last few weeks. Did something happen?"

I shook my head and dodged the question. "I've just been really busy with the musical, and they're not really into that." Part of me wanted to tell them, but I didn't know where to start. What would they do? It's not like their knowing would change anything. Not really. Suddenly I had an inspiration. "I've been thinking about taking up taekwondo. Shanika, the one who plays Tiger Lily, is a black belt, and she said there's a camp over spring break I could go to."

Mom and Dad both let out a sigh of relief. "I think that's a great idea!" Dad exclaimed.

Mom hesitated. "I think maybe we better have the doctor take a look, just to make sure you're okay first."

"Ah, Mom," I whined. "I'm okay. I don't need to see a doctor."

"Maybe," Mom replied. "But I've already scheduled an appointment for you tomorrow morning."

I stared at her in disbelief. "You already made an appointment?" I felt a sudden flash of angry fear and bit my lower lip. "So when were you planning on telling me?"

"Right now," Dad said. "That's why we're having this discussion."

Mom nodded. "I've cleared my morning calendar so I can take you. The appointment's at 7:30, so you shouldn't miss much school." My parents always liked to get the first appointment of the day before anybody had a chance to get behind.

"What doctor?" I asked, wondering whether it would be the pediatrician that I hadn't seen since I was ten or the family doctor I'd never seen at all. I really hadn't been to the doctor for anything except what the school required, and I did all of that at the clinics.

"Dr. Parks," Mom said. "I think it's time for you to start going to our family doctor."

"It's much easier to get an appointment there than at the pediatrician's office," Dad added. "Maybe he can rule out mono and give you a clean bill of health to start this taekwondo class you're interested in."

I went up to my room and texted Troy. "I don't need a ride to school 2mRO."

He texted me back. "K."

I waited for him to ask me why not, but he didn't. My phone was silent. Finally, I texted him again. "I have a Dr. appt."

"U OK?"

I thought about it. What was I supposed to say? "Yeah, I'll tell you later."

"K."

The next morning Mom and I arrived at Dr. Parks' office a few minutes before the doors opened. When we walked into the abandoned waiting room, I went straight for a chair in the far corner. Mom checked in with the receptionist and filled out all of the paperwork. I had stuffed a small water bottle filled with vodka into the very bottom of the side pocket of my back pack, but I didn't dare pull it out while I was with Mom.

I dreaded seeing the doctor. I'd had only one gulp of vodka and a dose of Nyquil to steady my nerves. I brought the Nyquil with me, too, but I wasn't supposed to have it at school. There wasn't much in it, though, so I figured I could go to the bathroom, down the rest of the bottle and throw it in the trash. I became increasingly fidgety as the waiting room filled with patients. I fiddled with a box of crème-de-menthe flavored Altoids I bought at the grocery store last night before popping two in my mouth at the same time.

I was still sucking on the Altoids when the doctor started feeling around on my lymph nodes and wanted to take a look at my throat. Just as Mom said, "Spit those things out," I swallowed, and down they went.

"They're gone," I said, opening my mouth wide and letting the doctor push down my tongue with a wooden tongue depressor. Then he put on a glove and grabbed my tongue, twisting it up and down and all around while I did my best to suppress the glugging and gurgling noises. He had me lay down and poked around at my liver and spleen. Then he sent me out to empty my bladder in a specimen cup.

When I returned he was sitting on his little rolling stool, swiveling gently back and forth as Mom recounted my symptoms over the past few weeks. I could feel him staring at me. "I don't think it's mono," he said, "but we'll run some tests and see what we come up with. I'd like to get a blood sample, too." He turned to Mom. "You can wait here while I walk Sandy down to the phlebotomist." Then he turned to me. "Come with me, Sandy."

I followed the doctor down the hall and into a cluttered office. "Have a seat," he said, pointing to a chair in front of a desk heaped with papers and files while he took a seat behind the desk. "Your mom says you've had fatigue and flu-like symptoms for several weeks." I nodded. "You're 16?" I nodded again. "Sandy, I brought you down here because I want to ask you something straight up, and I want you to be able to answer me without worrying about what your mom might think."

Instant anxiety seized every cell of my body. I could not meet Dr. Parks' eyes. I fixed my eyes on the floor and held my breath.

"I smelled alcohol when I was examining your tongue and throat. That's not something I would expect to smell on the breath of a teenager at 8:00 in the morning."

"Maybe it was the Altoids," I offered. "They're crème-de-menthe flavor."

"Maybe. The urine and blood tests will tell me if I'm wrong. I just wanted to give you the chance to tell me about it now if it's going to show up on these tests."

I continued to stare at the floor.

"Is there any chance that I'll find alcohol in your blood or urine?"

I winced. "Maybe," I stammered. "Maybe there's alcohol in the Nyquil I took."

"Your mom didn't say anything about your taking Nyquil."

"She doesn't know. I have the bottle in my backpack." I felt a huge rush of relief as the story just seemed to flow. "I bought it at the grocery store because it's for the flu. I'm not supposed to take it to school, but it's almost gone. I was going to take the rest of it before I got to school and throw it away before I went in the building. I just wanted to feel better so my parents would let me start taking taekwondo with a friend of mine over spring break."

I looked up at the doctor. He was rubbing his chin. "Are you taking it as directed?"

I nodded. "Do you think that's what's making me tired?"

"I don't know," Dr. Parks replied. "What do you think?"

I tried to look him in the eye, but I just couldn't do it. I shrugged my shoulders and looked away.

"Your symptoms sound a lot like depression to me. Is there anything bothering you?"

Part of me wanted to tell him, to just say it. But my throat was tightening, and my eyes were getting watery, and the words simply wouldn't come. "I'm just tired," I finally mumbled.

The doctor waited a long time before he said, "No more Nyquil. Let's get the blood drawn, and then we'll throw away whatever's in your backpack."

"Are you going to tell my mom?" I asked.

"Not if you tell her first."

12

And thus I clothe my naked villainy
With old odd ends stolen out of Holy Writ
And seem a saint, when most I play the devil.

—*Richard III*, Act I, Scene iii, Lines 336-338

I TOLD MOM about the Nyquil with Dr. Parks standing right there. Then I told Dad about the Nyquil while Mom listened. And by the time I was finished telling, it was all about the Nyquil and the flu and my just wanting to sign up for this taekwondo class, but thinking my parents wouldn't let me because I was already busy with the school musical.

"I'll drive you to school tomorrow and Friday," Dad said. It wasn't open for discussion.

"And no more Nyquil," Mom said. "When you think you need medicine, we need to know."

"No more Nyquil," I promised. My parents seemed satisfied. It was an easy promise to keep. Nobody said anything about vodka. That would have been a problem. I tried not to think about that. Spring break would be here soon enough. Maybe taekwondo would help me feel relaxed and more focused again, too, like it did for Shanika.

That night I got a text from Troy. "What did Dr. say?"

"Just needed a physical for taekwondo over spring break."

"Taekwondo?"

"Why not, right?" I texted back.

"See you in the morning?"

"Dad wants to drive me the rest of this week."

"K."

And that was it. I tried not to think about it.

Just when I was getting good at not thinking, Mr. Conaway decided that we should study Socrates in our AP World History class. "The Socratic Method is a favorite with teachers, philosophers and lawyers," he said. Then we spent the whole period discussing a single question: "What is Virtue?"

There was lots of talk about vice and virtue and right and wrong. I sat quietly in my seat avoiding teacher eye contact. Eventually, though, Mr. Conaway asked me directly, "What do you think about virtue, Sandy?"

"Some rise by sin, and some by virtue fall," I replied.

Mr. Conaway laughed. "Shakespeare, I presume?"

I nodded. "*Measure for Measure*."

"But what does it mean?"

I shrugged. "I guess it means that sometimes people succeed by doing the wrong thing, and some people fail even though they've done everything the right way."

"Do you think that's true?" Mr. Conaway asked.

Hands shot up all over the classroom. The whole thing turned into a debate on whether it's better to do the right thing for the wrong reasons or the wrong thing for the right reasons. I just stayed out of it. *Nothing is right. It's all wrong. What's wrong with me?*

Then came our spring break assignment. "Pick one of the questions and really think about it," Mr. Conaway instructed as he handed out a long list of questions like "What is Justice?" and "What is Truth?"

"Just think about it?" someone asked.

"Think about it, and then write about it in a way that lets me know you've given the question serious thought," Mr. Conaway replied.

"How long does it have to be?" inquired another student.

"Doesn't matter," said Mr. Conaway. "There's no right answer and no right length."

This created quite a stir. "Does that mean you're not going to grade us?"

"You'll definitely be getting a grade on this assignment."

Amy Taylor's hand shot up. Her one and only goal in life was to be class valedictorian. "How can you grade us on something that doesn't have a right answer and you won't even tell us how long the answer needs to be?"

"Let me just tell you that the more 'canned' your answer sounds, the less inclined I'll be to give you a good grade."

"But that's not fair!" Amy argued. "You have to tell us what you want us to do!"

"I want you to think for yourself, Amy. Look at the list of questions. See number 12?"

Amy nodded. "It says, 'What is Fair?'"

Mr. Conaway smiled. "There you go."

The class laughed and started whispering back and forth about the different questions. I scanned through the list: "What is

Good?" "What is Freedom?" What is Life?" "What is Integrity?" Finally, I saw one that captured my attention. "What is Character?" *Character is whatever role I choose to play. There you go. That one should be easy enough for a character actor who knows how to stay in character.*

Aside from that single assignment, my spring break was all about taekwondo. Sarah Hensley and Dustin Fairbanks would be out of town all week, so Hamilton wasn't planning any serious rehearsals without Wendy and Captain Hook. Of course, we could always come in several hours a day to work on sets or to go over our part with Hamilton privately. And he encouraged the understudies to work on their parts together if they were around. My plan was to follow Shanika's lead. If she found time to go in, I would too. If not, then so be it.

That Friday when school let out, Dad took me to my first taekwondo class and got me signed up for the spring break camp. It sounds crazy, but the moment I stepped into the Washington do-jahng, I felt safer than I'd felt in weeks. I had to swallow hard to keep back the tears. Shanika introduced me to her father and then showed me around the facility while my dad completed all of the paperwork and paid for the course.

There was a black belt class in progress, and I watched as they did punches and kicks with great energy and precision. They were mostly teenagers, but several younger kids and adults were mixed in as well. Age, height and athletic ability didn't seem to have anything to do with who stood where. Without warning, the whole class gave a loud shout in unison that startled me so badly I jumped and yelled, too.

Shanika laughed, but not in a mean way. "That's a kiyap. It's part of the forms. You'll get used to it."

She picked out a uniform for me and then showed me how to tie the belt once I had it on. She taught me how to bow when you enter and leave the do-jahng and also when you step on and off the mat where class is held. Then she had me take a seat while she joined the black belt class.

The whole class stood at attention while Shanika introduced me. "This is my friend, Sandy." The entire class turned and bowed in my direction and then shouted, "ATA." From all of the signs and posters I gathered that stood for the American Taekwondo Association. Then she turned to me. "Sandy, this is the white belt form you'll be learning at the rank-advancement camp." She turned back to the class and ordered them all to do the same form.

It was like synchronized martial arts. People in all sizes, shapes and colors moved together with a shared confidence. All wore perfectly pressed white uniforms with patches on their sleeves and black belts wrapped around their waists. I looked down at my white belt—white for purity. There was a poster on the wall explaining all of the different color belts and their meaning. Beside the white belt were the words, "Pure and without the knowledge of Songahm Taekwondo. As with the Pine Tree, the seed must now be planted and nourished to develop strong roots."

Shanika called for everyone to put on their sparring gear. A vast array of padding, helmets, and mouth guards exploded from behind the counter and loud music blared from a boom box. As I watched the students pair up and begin sparring I suddenly imagined myself sparring Aaron. *So much padding and protection. It would be almost impossible for him to slip his hand* . . . I shuddered at the thought.

I swallowed the panic and blinked back the tears. *Take a drink. Don't take a drink.* I looked at Dad who was still talking to Mr. Washington. *Take a quick drink. No one will notice.* I looked at Shani-

ka who was stepping right into the line of fire between two sparring men. *Don't take a drink. Wait until after class.* Only right after this
black belt class was the class I would be attending. *Just a little drink
now and a real drink after class.* So I took a quick little drink, and no
one seemed to notice.

At the end of the black belt class, everyone bowed to Shanika,
and a cheerful chorus rang out, "Ma'am! I shall live with perseverance in the spirit of taekwondo, having honor with others, integrity
for myself, and self-control in my actions, Ma'am!" *Honor. Integrity.
Self-control. All the things I took for granted. Everything I've lost.* I sucked
in a deep breath and followed a line of students wearing white, orange and yellow belts onto the mat for my first taekwondo class.

13

Like a dull actor now
I have forgot my part and I am out
Even to a full disgrace.

—*Coriolanus*, Act V, Scene iii, Lines 40-42

I WAS A little worried about how to manage my schedule during the camp and make it to the store to pick up a bottle when I needed it. So I decided to stock up over the weekend. I even managed to walk out with two bottles from the same store in a single visit. A huge burden lifted as I lined up my three bottles of vodka in my closet that Sunday night.

Once I was sure my parents were in bed, I poured a glass of vodka and pulled out my World History assignment sheet. *What is character? What is integrity?* I stared at the paper and tried to think. I pictured myself at the do-jahng with my white belt. *Honor. Integrity. Self-control. Right.*

My thoughts kept taking me back to that one minute that absolutely destroyed everything inside me. How could my whole world change in a moment and without anyone else knowing? At some level I knew that Aaron's actions defined him, not me, but it didn't change how totally broken I felt inside. I took another drink and started doodling in my notebook. Doodling and scribbling and drinking. This was getting me nowhere.

I went to the bathroom and splashed cold water on my face. I stared at myself in the mirror for a really long time. My pupils were dilated, and my eyes had a cloudy look to them. I tried to look deeper, but it was no use. My eyes were nothing but black holes . . . little windows to the interminable darkness inside me. I went back to my room and took another drink.

Then I started scratching out a poem of sorts about character. I worked it and reworked it until I felt totally spent and the mess of scribbles was nearly unintelligible. So I recopied it on a clean page:

My Character

Every day I face frustration
Confusing discontent
But it doesn't seem to matter
All the wasted time I've spent

Pretending to be someone
When I know it's just a game
Changing scenes and changing roles
But still it's all the same

I've read the script before
A play is all that life will be
Unless I find the character
I know is really me

Enough. I lay down on my bed and fell asleep.

I began the rank advancement camp with a sense of adventure. Kids of all ages lined up in descending order according to belt colors. As the newest white belt at the school, I was always last in the line. I recognized a few faces, but Shanika was the only one I really knew. She always lined up with the instructors, facing the students.

One of the orange belts was a guy from my class at school named Hector Quintana. I faintly remembered his being a wrestler in middle school, and that made me a little uneasy somehow. But by the end of the first day, it was obvious he was nothing at all like Aaron, and I stopped feeling so jittery around him.

Overall, taekwondo really seemed to calm my mind. By concentrating on each movement in the form and executing each step with physical precision, I felt the tension in every cell of my body begin to release. I didn't need the vodka quite so much. Instead of drinking alone in my room, I practiced white belt form and sparring one-steps over and over again in my mind. I even went all day Wednesday without taking a drink. I had it with me, but I never actually needed it.

Then came Thursday. After camp, Mr. Washington asked Shanika to run to the grocery store to pick up some refreshments for a rank-advancement celebration on Friday. Shanika asked me to go with her. I called Dad to let him know Shanika would bring me home later.

We split up while we were in the store, each gathering some of the items her dad wanted. I walked through the liquor section by myself and felt really good about the fact that I wasn't there to steal anything. My backpack felt especially light. I headed back through the school supply aisle and picked up another spiral notebook for myself; then I joined Shanika in the check-out line, putting all of the taekwondo things I'd gathered into her shopping cart.

Shanika waited for me to pay for the notebook, and we walked out of the store together. The moment I stepped through the door, though, a big guy in khakis and a polo shirt that said STORE SECURITY stepped in front of me, blocking my way. He startled me so badly that I couldn't stop shaking.

"Hey!" Shanika cried, letting go of her cart and trying to step between us. "What do you think you're doing?"

The security guard pushed her aside. "You're free to go." Then he pressed his finger into my chest and said, "You're coming with me."

"But we're together!" I heard Shanika argue.

"Fine," said the security guard. "You can both come with me." He took me by the arm and escorted me back into the store. Shanika followed closely behind. There was a loud rattling. I knew it was the wheels on the grocery cart, but it felt more like every bone in my body.

The security guard led us back into an office where a woman wearing a STORE MANAGER pin-on tag was waiting for us. She looked surprised to see Shanika. The woman sat behind a desk next to a television, and there were several TV monitors beside the television showing different areas of the store. My eyes fixed on the one surveying the liquor aisle.

"Hand me your backpack," the man commanded.

Without a word, I removed the pack from my back. My hands shook visibly as I handed it to him. I knew he wouldn't find what he was looking for, but there was a little water bottle half-filled with vodka.

"Now sit down," he ordered. He glared at Shanika. "I suppose you can stand there if you like." He pointed to a corner behind me. I wasn't sure whether it was better for Shanika to stay or go, but if she was going to stay, I really wanted her someplace where I could see her.

The store manager sat at the desk calmly filling out paperwork while the security guard rummaged through my backpack. "Nothing!" he muttered. He tossed the backpack into my lap.

"Doesn't matter," replied the manager. She handed me a form that consisted of several different colored sheets bonded together at the top. "Fill out the first part," she instructed. Then she motioned to Shanika. "What about her? Did you see her take anything?" The security guard shook his head.

I could hear Shanika stirring behind me. "What's this all about? Sandy, you don't have to do anything they tell you to do." The security guard swiftly escorted her out of the room. "Do you want me to call your mom?" Shanika called back to me. Shanika's voice began to fade as she walked away, but I could still hear her verbally assaulting the security guard. "She's a lawyer, you know. You have no idea who you're messing with!"

I filled out my name, address and age on the form entitled No Trespass Notice. I handed the completed form back to the store manager.

"Do you want me to call your parents?" she asked as she took the form.

I shook my head.

"I have something I want to show you." She picked up a remote, pointed it toward the television and pushed the play button.

It wasn't very clear, and it wasn't very smooth, but I recognized the person picking up a bottle of vodka and scurrying down the aisle.

"Is that you?" the store manager asked. I didn't say anything.

"Maybe you'll remember this next one since it was taken just this past Saturday." Again she pushed the play button. It wasn't any clearer or any smoother, but there I was, picking up two bottles off the shelf and hurrying away.

I still didn't say anything. I knew from years of listening to my mom talk about her clients that I had the right to remain silent. The worst thing I could do was to admit that was me in the videos.

"Is there anything you have to say for yourself?" the woman asked.

I held my tongue.

"Fine. Have it your way." The woman carefully tore the back sheet off the form and handed me the pink copy of the NO TRES-PASS NOTICE. "You are no longer welcome in any of our stores. If you so much as set foot in the parking lot of any one of our stores again, I'll have you arrested for trespassing. Do you understand?"

I nodded.

"Now take your backpack and your bag and get out of here."

I walked out of the office and out of the store. Shanika was standing in the parking lot beside her car arguing loudly with the security guard. The security guard held an empty grocery cart between them. When she saw me approaching she gave the cart a push and shouted, "Well, it's about time!"

When the security guard saw me walking toward them with the pink paper in my hand, he said, "I dare you to come back here, you little snot." He rammed the cart into one of the metal holding areas and marched back into the store.

I climbed into the car and slammed the door. Shanika was ranting, but I only shook my head. "Just get me out of here," I pleaded. She nodded, and we drove away.

14

Confess yourself to Heaven,
Repent what's past, avoid what is to come,
And do not spread the compost on the weeds
To make them ranker.

—*Hamlet*, Act III, Scene iv, Lines 149-152

WE DROVE BACK to the taekwondo studio in silence. I reached inside my backpack, pulled out the small water bottle, and took a serious gulp of vodka to calm my nerves. Shanika parked the car near the door, but we didn't get out.

"Are you going to tell me what this is all about?" she asked.

I handed her the pink NO TRESPASS NOTICE.

She read it carefully before handing it back to me. "Why are they treating you like a shoplifter? Better yet, why are you letting them?"

I took another drink from the small water bottle and handed it to her.

"You stole a little bottle of water?" she asked incredulously.

I shook my head. "Smell it."

Shanika put it up to her nose. "It smells like alcohol."

I nodded, taking the bottle from her hands. "I stole a bottle of vodka."

"What!" Shanika exclaimed. She pounded the steering wheel with both hands. "Are you crazy? You walked in that store with me and instead of takin' care of business, you're stealin' vodka? I am so going to kick your butt!"

I shook my head. "Not today. Over the weekend. That's why they stopped me today. After you left they showed me the surveillance video." I sighed. For a moment I thought having Shanika literally kick my butt might actually make me feel better. I closed my eyes. *Bam! Bam! Bam! It would feel so good to be knocked senseless.*

"You have some serious explaining to do." She paused. "Sandy, look at me." I steeled myself and looked directly in her eyes. "Why are you stealing vodka?"

I shook my head and looked away again. "Because I'm not old enough to buy it?" I closed my eyes waiting for her to knife-hand strike me. *Just hit me. We'll both feel better if you do.*

"Very funny. I'm serious, Sandy. When did you start drinking?"

Tears filled my eyes, but my throat wasn't swelling shut. I turned back to face Shanika and in that instant, I knew that I was going to tell her. I was going to tell her everything, even if she didn't believe me and even if it meant she never spoke to me again.

I wiped the tears from my eyes and inhaled all of the sniffles from my nose. "The Ides of March," I said. "March 15 . . . " I let my voice trail off. Shanika waited. I took a deep breath. *Just say it. Just tell her what happened.* Again I turned away, just to swallow the sob that wanted to leap from my throat.

Shanika put one hand on my shoulder and used the other to gently turn my face back toward her. I didn't resist. "Sandy, what happened on March 15?"

I kept my eyes tightly closed. My jaw trembled. My lower lip quivered. I forced myself to take a deep breath and finally blurted out the awful truth. "Aaron Jackson sexually assaulted me."

"Oh my God," Shanika whispered. She dropped her hands into her lap. This time she looked away. Finally, she turned back to me. "Did you tell anyone?"

I shook my head. "I tried to tell Cassie, but Aaron already fed her some line. She thinks I'm making a big deal out of nothing."

"What about your parents? The police?"

I shook my head. "It happened so fast. Nobody will believe me." I gave her a weak smile. "I decided it would be better just to act like nothing happened."

"Well, I believe you," Shanika declared. "And drinking yourself silly isn't going to help."

I shrugged my shoulders and took another drink from the bottle.

"Sandy!"

I leaned my head back and closed my eyes feeling the soothing warmth of the alcohol surging through my arteries.

"I mean it, Sandy. We've got to do something about Aaron."

I looked at her blankly. "Us? You and me? What can we do?"

"We can call the police."

The thought made me shiver. "After what just happened? I don't think so."

"Well, we have to tell somebody." She looked around the car and then after the window. "You can tell your parents. Your mom's a lawyer. She'll know what to do."

"Right. My mom represents people like Aaron and gets them off." I looked at the bottle in my hand. "Plus, if I tell my parents I'll have to tell them everything . . . the drinking . . . the stealing . . .

I'm just not ready to do that. I drained the last of the vodka from the bottle. "I'm really not ready to do that."

"Well, you can't keep stealing alcohol."

"I know. I was hoping you might know someone cool who was old enough to buy it for me."

Shanika shook her head. "That's no kind of a plan." She took the empty bottle from my hands and crumpled it up. "We can tell my dad."

"You think your dad would buy me alcohol?" I asked feeling suddenly hopeful.

"Forget the alcohol, Sandy. We can just tell my dad what happened."

"No way!" I cried. "Besides, even if he believed me, what could your dad do? Break every bone in Aaron's body?"

For a second I thought Shanika was going to cry. She put her hands over her face and rested her head on her palms, eyes covered, elbows propped on her thighs. "My dad would believe you, too," she said softly. "But I'm not sure what he could do, either."

Shanika appeared visibly shaken, and it made me uneasy. She looked like she was about to tell me something, but then she shook it off. I waited. When she turned to look me in the eyes, she said, "Sandy, I'm going to tell you something that I'm not supposed to know about."

A tingling sense of danger crept up my neck. I wished I had another bottle of vodka with me.

"You know Hector Quintana?"

I nodded.

"Well, he was on the wrestling team this year. He's pretty good for a sophomore and made varsity. Right before the first match, while he was getting dressed in the locker room, there was some sort of hazing incident."

"What's that got to do with me?" I asked.

"That's what I'm trying to tell you. The hazing thing was really a sexual assault. They took Hector's mouthpiece and shoved it 'where the sun don't shine.'"

I felt my eyes widen. "Aaron did that to Hector?"

"I don't think Aaron actually did it, but he's the captain of the team, and you know he was behind it."

I sat there stunned, trying to soak it all in and wondering what it all meant. "So what did Hector do?"

"He washed off his mouthpiece, pinned his opponent, and then quit the wrestling team."

I nodded. "And signed up for taekwondo."

"Yeah," Shanika replied. "Actually, I think he told his parents, and the taekwondo was his parents' idea."

"Wow," I said. "I never would have thought that about Hector."

"Well, you just never know, do you?" said Shanika. "And anyway, this isn't about Hector. This is about Aaron." She pounded the steering wheel with her fists. "Somebody really needs to do something about that guy!" She sounded so angry. It was the most anger I'd ever experienced in such tight quarters.

I didn't know what to say. "He just thinks he's such a stud," I offered.

"Aaron's no stud. He thinks he can hide behind that hard-on, but it's not about sex, Sandy. It's really not . . . not the hazing, not the rape, not the assault . . . it's pure violence. The cruelest kind of violence.

It seemed funny the way she said the word *rape*. "I don't think it was really rape, what Aaron did to me. Or to Hector."

But Shanika didn't answer. She seemed suddenly lost in another world. I waited several moments before switching the conversation back to Hector. "Did Hector's parents report the incident to the school or the police?" I asked.

"I don't know," Shanika admitted. "I guess not because it doesn't look like anybody's doing anything about it." She hesitated. And then her voice dropped so low I almost didn't hear her. "Just because you tell them doesn't mean they'll do anything about it."

I gave her shoulder a playful push. "That's not making me want to tell," I said. "And anyway, I feel a little better just knowing that you know. Give me some time. I'll think about it."

Shanika nodded. "Yeah, better to think about it. Don't tell just because I want you to. You decide for yourself. I'm here for you either way." She looked at me and smiled. Then she broke into our favorite musical number. "You just send for Tiger Lily. I'll just send for Peter Pan," she sang.

I joined in, "We'll be coming willy, nilly, Lily."

Shanika nodded. "Beat on a drum, and I will come."

15

"Dive, thoughts, down to my soul."

—*Richard III*, Act I, Scene i, Line 41

THAT NIGHT ALONE in my room, I drank. I tried to pace myself, but I had to keep drinking. All of the shock I'd felt initially had finally worn off. The only thing I could feel was the raw pain of the violation. *The violence.* Even the vodka couldn't seem to take the edge off of that excruciating pain.

At first, telling Shanika was a relief. It somehow helped to know that she knew and that she believed me. But now, all alone again, I wanted to take it all back. Somehow her knowing made it all the more real. There seemed to be this long row of people lined up like dominoes . . . Shanika's dad, my dad, my mom, Troy, the police, the school, everybody at school, Hector . . . Telling Shanika, just Shanika, was like pushing that very first domino. They were all going to fall.

But maybe, just maybe, Shanika was strong enough to stand this. Maybe she really wouldn't tell her dad or anybody. *But if I show up at taekwondo tomorrow all drunk or hung-over, that will push her over for sure.* I had to stop drinking. I put the vodka away and chugged down a big bottle of water. *That's it. No room for any more liquid.* But I felt all knotted up and queasy.

I grabbed the notebook I'd written the poem in Sunday night and started writing down the words that came to mind. It helped to just put them out there and stare at them.

Cassie   Aaron   Sex
Hector   Aaron   Violence
What about me?
Why me?
It's not about sex.

I stared at that page a long time. Finally, I flipped to a new page and just started writing as fast as the thoughts came to me.

Violence is violence
It's not about sex
It's power and anger and fear

Friendship is friendship
I thought it would last
Year after year after year

School is school
Get me out of this place
Just let me become Peter Pan

My life is a mess
I can't take anymore
I'm doing the best that I can

Sex is just sex
A three-letter word
Take it or leave it alone

And God, where is God?
There's a three-letter word
Designed to condemn or condone

HELP—I need help
But who can I trust?
And how do I deal with the pain?

HOPE—Is there hope?
Will this night never end?
I'm gradually going insane

I put down my pen and realized all of the pressure had moved from my head to my bladder. *Too much real water.* I closed the notebook, went to the bathroom and then totally crashed on my bed.

I was so crashed that my mom had to shake me awake the next morning. It startled me so that I woke up screaming, which totally freaked my mom out and then she was yelling, and Dad came running up the stairs to see what was wrong, and there I was, still in my clothes from the night before and drenched in sweat.

"It was just a nightmare," I told them.

"Probably brought on by fever," Mom said, feeling my damp forehead and wet clothes. "It seems to have broken now, though."

She sent my dad for the thermometer and sat on the edge of my bed stroking my cheek. It made me want to cry so bad that I had to turn over on my side away from her. She gently rubbed my back until Dad returned.

"Let me take your temperature," she said. She sniffled a little bit and her eyes glistened with tears. As we waited for the thermometer to beep, she said softly, "I just wish I knew what was going on with you, Sandy."

When she took the thermometer from my mouth, she read it silently and then handed it to Dad. "No fever," he said. "That's good, right?"

I sat up in bed and rubbed my eyes with my sleeve. "Good. Today's the last day of camp, and I wouldn't want to miss it."

"Do you think we should call Dr. Parks?" Dad asked.

Mom hesitated; so I answered, "I don't. It was just a bad dream. It's over." Mom still didn't look convinced. "I don't even remember what it was now," I added.

"Sandy, when was the last time you took Nyquil?" Dad asked.

"I haven't taken any since we went to see Dr. Parks. Honest."

"Are you taking anything else?" Mom asked.

Ooh, trickier question. I've been taking alcohol from the grocery store, but that was last weekend. "Mo-om," I tried to sound incredulous. "I've been in taekwondo camp all week. The last thing I drank was a bottle of water," I said picking up the empty bottle and handing it to her.

She lifted it to her nose and then handed it to Dad. "What?" he asked.

"It's water," she said.

Dad looked completely baffled. "Of course it's water."

I held my breath. The thought of Mom sniffing all of my water bottles sent adrenaline surging through every muscle in my body.

"Speaking of taekwondo, I'd better go. I'm testing for orange belt this morning." I got up and started getting my clothes around.

"Wait, Sandy," Mom said. She and Dad were making funny faces back and forth in some secret communication effort. I remember when I was really little and they used to spell back and forth when they didn't want me to know what they were talking about. When I could follow them no matter how fast they spelled, they started using Latin phrases. Once I started picking up on those, they've invented some weird secret facial expressions or something. But I wasn't sure they really ever knew what the other one was trying to convey any better than I did.

Mom was patting on the bed like she wanted me to sit back down. "Wait for what?" I asked slowly, reluctant to sit back down on the bed now that I was up. "I need to use the bathroom and jump in the shower."

"I want you to talk to a counselor," she said. "I feel like you're worried about something and for whatever reason you don't want to talk to us about it. But you need to talk to someone."

I tried to shrug it off like it was no big deal. "Fine. I'll talk to a counselor. Whatever. Can I go now?" I didn't actually wait for her to answer.

I swallowed a couple of Tylenol from the bottle we kept in the medicine cabinet, then took a long shower, wasting more time and more water than usual, and thinking about what it would be like to see a counselor. *It might not be bad, especially with the whole shoplifting thing out there. When the police come knocking on our door, maybe the counselor can explain to my parents how everything can get so crazy so fast. But, then again, I wouldn't want the counselor running back to my parents with everything I might say.*

By the time I came downstairs to have Dad drive me to taekwondo, I was feeling pretty good. My parents had made an appointment for me the following week with a Dr. McMann. Mom had already left for the office. Dad told me as we got into the car.

"Man or woman?" I asked.

"Does it matter?" he wanted to know.

"I guess not," I said. Suddenly I had this picture of a dark room with a couch—me lying on the couch . . . Aaron watching me. I pushed that image out of my head and tried to picture Dr. McMann. In popped this idea of me visiting some Ronald McDonald in a fast food Play Place. I smiled and shook my head.

"What's so funny?" Dad asked.

"It's just that McMann kind of sounds like a guy in a Ronald McDonald suit to me."

Dad laughed. "Then you'll be happy to know that Dr. McMann is a woman."

"No clown suit?" I asked.

"No clown suit," answered Dad. He had his eyes on the road, so I had a chance to really look at him. When I was a kid he seemed like the biggest, smartest, strongest person in the world. I really thought he knew everything. But now, he was still a good guy and all, he just seemed so clueless. It made me want to cry. I turned away and tried picturing a woman in the Ronald McDonald suit. But the humor was gone.

"So how'd you come up with her?" I asked.

"She's the best in town." The way he looked at me, it suddenly felt like he was saying I'm so messed up she's probably the only one who could help me. But then his face softened. "Your mom knows her. Says kids seem to like her . . . " His voice trailed off. "We just want whatever's best for you, Sandy."

"I know, Dad." I wanted to say *I'm okay* or at least *I'll be okay*, but it felt like a lie. So I just said, "It'll be okay." And we drove the rest of the way in silence.

16

Oh, what may man within him hide,
Though angel on the outward side!
How may likeness made in crimes,
Making practice on the times,
To draw with idle spider's strings
Most ponderous and substantial things!

—*Measure for Measure*, Act III, Scene ii, Lines 285-290

AS I GOT out of the car, I realized a whole week had passed since I'd seen or talked to Troy. More than that for Cassie. They hadn't even sent me as much as a short, "hey how r u" text message. It's like I was dead to them. Of course, I hadn't texted them either, but why would I since I was already dead to them? *They were never really my friends. What did we ever even have in common? Cassie's mom as a babysitter when we were in preschool. No wonder I don't miss them.* Except I did.

I bowed as I walked into the do-jahng. *These people are my friends now. Shanika. Hector.* Shanika and I had the musical and now taekwondo in common. Hector and I were in the same grade, and we had taekwondo. *And Aaron. No, not Aaron. Maybe too much in common.* Maybe actually being friends with Hector wasn't such a great idea. But at least I had Shanika. *As long as she doesn't mind being friends with a drunk and a thief.* Suddenly, I could hardly breathe.

I dropped my taekwondo bag inside the studio, then turned and ran back outside. Dad was already driving off, but I walked around the corner of the building and out of sight just in case. I leaned forward with my hands on my knees, gasping for breath like I'd just run a four-minute mile. I straightened myself and tried to walk it off, holding my side and taking slow, deep breaths. My eyes were wet with tears. I walked around to the back of the building where there was a picnic table and water fountain.

I took a drink of water and remembered that I hadn't brought any vodka with me today. Before I knew it, I was crying and trembling and trying to figure out how I was ever going to walk back into the studio, let alone test for orange belt. I sat down on top of the picnic table with my feet on the seat. I folded my arms across my knees, put my head down and let myself have a really good cry.

When it felt like all of the tears were out, I got another drink of water from the fountain and splashed the cold water all over my face and in my eyes. Then I stood up straight, focused and took a deep breath. *See-jup. Your form, your count.* And I started doing white belt form with every ounce of energy and precision I could muster. It felt good—really good—just to move my whole body with such purpose.

When I was finished and turned back toward the building, I saw Shanika standing there. "You okay?"

I nodded. "Just getting ready for testing."

"Your form looks good, but you're late." She motioned for me to follow her into the back door of the building. "There's no testing outside."

"At least my bag was on time."

95

Shanika laughed. "Yeah, and how many of the eighteen white belt moves do you think your bag has done while you were out here?"

"I don't know," I said smiling. "How many moves did you teach it?"

"You're crazy, Sandy, you know that?"

I nodded. "My parents think so, too." I dropped my voice as we walked through the back storage room toward the main studio. "They made an appointment for me to see a counselor next week."

Shanika stopped. "No kidding?"

"No kidding."

"Do they know?" she asked.

"I don't think so." We were standing in between two kicking dummies and I couldn't resist throwing a couple of punches to this rubber green guy's head. "I'm pretty sure they would have told me, though, if they'd gotten a call from the store or from the police."

"Not that!" Shanika smacked the back of the dummy's head at the same time I threw another punch, and it sent the shock of my blow right back up my arm. "I mean did you tell them about Aaron."

I shook my head. "I haven't told them anything. They just know something's up."

"So they're sending you to some psycho therapist?"

I nodded. "Come on. I'm late, remember?"

She smacked herself in the forehead. "Duh! Let's go. We can talk about this later. Right now you need to focus on testing."

"That's what I thought."

Everyone was already lined up on the mat and clapping in unison as Shanika and I bowed and entered the testing area. I took my place at the back of the class with the other white belts and Shanika stood beside her father at the front of the class.

Mr. Washington bowed us all in and then explained how we would proceed, from white belts all the way up to red belts. There wouldn't be anyone testing for black belt, because you had to do that at a formal testing with several high-ranking black belts as judges. Once you got up to camo belt, the testing included sparring, and once you got up to brown belt, you had to do board breaking, too.

Even though all of the forms and everything got more difficult as you advanced, Mr. Washington said that white belt testing was the hardest because it was the first time you had everyone watching you with the pressure of performing each move accurately. "Once you have earned your orange belt, you have the confidence of knowing for certain that you can do this, one step at a time. Your instructor would not allow you to test if you weren't ready."

I was glad white belt testing came first. I was done in no time and able to watch all of the higher ranks without having to worry about forgetting my own form. And I'll admit, the person I watched most closely was Hector. He had his orange belt and was testing for his yellow belt.

Hector seemed to get lost at one point in the middle of his form. He just stood there for a moment, and I thought maybe he would give up or have to start over, but he didn't. Even when everyone else had finished, and the whole place was waiting on him, he didn't let it rattle him. I could tell he was mentally going through all of the moves in his mind and then when he caught up again with where he had stopped, he continued. And when he finished, the whole place applauded. Not just for him, but for all of the orange belts that were on the floor. But Hector was smiling like it was all just for him.

He did all of his one-step sparring segments with confidence. I looked around the room and wondered if anyone else knew he'd been assaulted. *Probably not. You wouldn't know if Shanika hadn't told you, and Shanika wouldn't even know if she hadn't overheard it.* No one except Shanika knew that I'd been assaulted. *Aaron knows what he did. Yeah, well, not like he's going to tell anyone.* No one except Shanika knew that I was a thief and a drunk. *Except maybe the people at the store. And maybe the police. Would they turn the videos over to the police?*

By the time testing was finished and we were reciting the honor, integrity and self-control pledge at the end, I was kind of glad that I was going to see a therapist. I thought about the way Shanika had said it. *Psycho therapist. Maybe if the woman is totally psycho, she'll at least understand how I feel.*

17

To be, or not to be—that is the question.
Whether 'tis nobler in the mind to suffer
The slings and arrows of outrageous fortune
Or to take arms against a sea of troubles
And by opposing end them. To die, to sleep—

—*Hamlet*, Act III, Scene i, Lines 58-60

SHANIKA DROVE ME home after the testing, and we had a chance to talk. I really wanted to ask her what she was doing this weekend and see if maybe we could just hang out sometime, but I was kind of afraid to ask, and she didn't offer.

"Thanks for the ride," I said as I got out of the car.

"See you Monday," she called back to me, and drove away.

So long, Shanika. So long, spring break. I stood there waving quite a bit longer than I should have. Definitely longer than I would have if Mom or Dad had been home. But they wouldn't be home from work for several hours yet. Which left me with nothing to do, except work on my AP World History assignment: What is character?

I pondered this question as I pulled out the three vodka bottles I had hidden in my closet, one full, one mostly full and one empty. Just looking at them made my mouth water and my stomach tighten. *To drink or not to drink—THAT is the real question.* On the one hand, I really wanted a drink to help me relax and get the creative juices flowing. On the other hand, I didn't know how long this vodka needed to last. My days of just walking out of a store with a bottle were over.

And what about character? Does character allow me to take a drink or no? What about the character I'm playing? Does the character I'm playing take a drink? What is character really?

I pulled out my phone and searched the internet for "character." Turns out the dictionary had more than a dozen definitions. I read through all of them. The only thing that spoke to me was the phrase "out of character." *That's me. Out of character. My character is gone. Drinking and stealing and feeling totally defeated . . . none of that is me. Where did it come from? Who am I becoming?*

I wasn't getting any closer to writing anything down for my assignment. Back to my real question of the moment: To drink or not to drink? Is it nobler to suffer all of the slings and arrows of my outrageous fortune or should I pick up the bottle and calm my sea of troubles?

I'm not a drunk. I don't have to drink. Except for last night, I haven't had hardly anything to drink all this whole week. But I'm feeling really thirsty now. Just don't think about it. Think about something else.

I started thinking about talking to Dr. McMann. What would I tell her? Where would I start? Who was she, anyway? I looked her up on the internet. The address popped up first. Her office was downtown, close to where my mom worked. I clicked on the link to her web page. This is what I saw: DR. ERIN MCMANN, PSYD, HSPP, ABPP across the top of the page. Underneath that was a headshot of Dr. McMann and underneath that were the words: PSYCHOLOGIST — THERAPIST.

First I focused on her name. Erin. Then the word THERAPIST jumped out at me. *Oh, my God, I don't believe it. I really don't believe it.*

I opened the mostly full bottle of vodka and took three swallows straight down. I stopped at three because I wasn't actually sure that last one was going down. My eyes watered and my nose burned. I coughed and gagged and looked at the web page again. Unbelievable. I turned the phone off and threw it on my bed.

I picked up my spiral notebook and turned to a clean page. I wrote "Erin" and "Therapist" across the top. I poured some vodka in a glass and took a drink. I don't know how long I sat there staring at the words. Finally, beneath them I wrote: "Erin" and "The rapist." *Of all the counselors in the world, my parents are sending me to Erin TheRapist.*

I had to get out of there before my parents came home. I carefully filled a water bottle with vodka to take with me and hid the rest. After much thought, I turned to a clean page in my notebook and wrote, "Meeting Hector at the library to work on history assignment." I signed my name, tore the page out of my notebook, put the notebook and bottle of vodka in my backpack, and left the note on the kitchen counter on my way out.

Maybe I will go to the library. My parents wouldn't worry if they thought I was at the library studying with someone. They knew my only assignment over spring break was a history assignment. They knew Shanika, Troy and Cassie weren't in my AP World History class, but all they knew about Hector is that we were in the same grade and that we both did the taekwondo rank advancement camp this week. They didn't know he wasn't actually in my AP World History class, but they also didn't know his parents well enough to just call them if they had a question like they might with Cassie's mom or Troy's dad. Plus, there are a dozen libraries in town. I could go to any one of them.

All I really wanted to do was walk. Just keep walking someplace where no one would notice me. Away from the university where my dad was. Away from downtown where my mom was. *And where Erin TheRapist has her office.* Without really meaning to I found myself walking back to the taekwondo place.

The studio was closed, so I just went around back to the picnic table. I set my backpack on the table, pulled out my water bottle and took another drink. Only I didn't really feel any relief. In fact, I think I actually felt worse. I screwed the top back on and set the bottle on the table next to my backpack. Then I started doing my white belt form. When I was done, I started all over. I did it again and again until I realized it was getting dark and also starting to cool down. I dug a sweatshirt out of my backpack and pulled it on.

I sat on the table in the dusk with my notebook and started to write.

I am everything.
I am nothing.
I could be anyone
Or no one at all.

I once had everything.
Now I have nothing.
I'm trapped in the darkness
Behind a brick wall.

What happened to everything?
I laugh and think nothing.
I'm not turning back.

I'm not willing to crawl.

Where is everybody?
Now that I'm nobody
All of my friends
Are just bricks in the wall.

I shoved my notebook back into my backpack. I needed a plan.
A plan to get through the night and the weekend. A plan to get
through my first session with Erin TheRapist. Mom's voice: *Well,
the first thing you can do is stop calling her that. Her name is Dr. McMann.* I
needed a plan to get through my first session with Dr. McMann or
to find another therapist. *The Rapist.* Counselor. I needed to find
another counselor. I lay down across the top of the table and using
my backpack as a pillow closed my eyes and went to sleep.

When I woke up it was dark, and there was someone shaking
me.

"No!" I shouted, struggling to get up and away.

"Sandy, it's okay." My eyes focused on Mr. Washington standing barefoot in his taekwondo uniform. "What are you doing
here?"

I stood up, but I couldn't think of anything to say. "I just . . . " I
started. Mr. Washington waited. "I don't know," I admitted. "I was
just looking for a place where I could think."

"Well, it's a little too cold and a little too dark for me to just
leave you out here thinking all night long. Come inside with me."
He motioned for me to follow him in the back door. We walked
through the same storage room I'd been in this morning, but it
seemed a lot darker and more ominous at night.

"I didn't think anyone was here," I said. I rubbed the green rubber dummy's six-pack abs for good luck as we walked past and into the dimly lit studio.

"I came back for a private lesson and was closing up shop for the weekend," he said. "I didn't think anyone else was here, either."

It felt weird being in the studio all alone with Mr. Washington. I wasn't afraid really, but I didn't feel like I belonged there anymore.

"Just have a seat over there while I finish up." Mr. Washington motioned to some stools by the counter. He erased the weekly white board calendar on the wall and wrote in the stuff for next week. "You got a car?" he asked when he was through.

"No, sir," I replied. Taekwondo was all about calling people "sir" and "ma'am." It seemed funny at first, especially calling Shanika "ma'am," but now I said it without thinking.

"So you want to tell me what you were thinking about?" Mr. Washington asked this kindly. He wasn't pressuring me, but I knew I couldn't tell him what I was really thinking about. So I decided to talk about the assignment.

"I have to do a paper on character," I said. "Due Monday."

"Well, I'm flattered that you came here." He smiled as he shuffled some papers into several stacks by the cash register. "So did you figure out what to write?"

I shook my head. "I ended up thinking more about honesty and integrity." *And self-control, only I don't want to say that out loud.*

"Maybe those have something to do with character," he said.

I nodded. "Do you ever talk to your taekwondo students about character?"

"Everything I teach my students is about character," he replied.

"So what would you say character is?" I asked.

"Oh, I'm better at just living what I think than I am at putting my thoughts into words." He came over beside me, pulled out another stool and sat down. "Did you ever hear of a guy called Wild Goose Jack?"

I shook my head.

"I didn't think so. I only heard of him because my grandmamma loved geese, especially the Canadian ones. Anyway, she told me Wild Goose Jack said that 'a man's reputation is what other people think of him; his character is what he really is.' I don't know if it's true, but it sounds good, and it's always stuck with me." He put his hand on my shoulder. "Come on, Sandy. I'll drive you home."

18

Be this the whetstone of your sword. Let grief
Convert to anger, blunt not the heart, enrage it.

—*Macbeth*, Act IV, Scene iii, Lines 228-229

MOM AND DAD were NOT happy when I walked in around 8:30 Friday night.

They both started talking at once. "We've been calling and texting for the past two hours!" "Who is this Hector? We don't want you driving around with people we haven't even met."

I slipped my backpack off and tried to calm them down. "Whoa, Mom. Dad. Didn't you get my note?"

"We got the note," Mom said.

"But we don't know anything at all about Hector," Dad cut in.

"And we would have liked to talk with you on the phone about it," Mom added.

"Where's your phone?" Dad asked.

I rummaged through my backpack. "I must have left it in my room. I'll go get it." I made a mad dash to get my backpack and vodka-filled water bottle as far from them as possible. I grabbed the phone off my bed and kicked my backpack under the bed and out of sight. Then I walked calmly back into the living room where they were arguing with each other. *Wow. I don't think I've ever heard them argue like this before.*

I sat down in the middle of the couch and waited until they stopped arguing with each other and turned their attention back to me. I checked my phone. Ten missed messages. "I'm really sorry," I said. "I passed my testing and earned my yellow belt. Then I re-membered about my paper due Monday, and decided to go to the library. Hector's in my grade at school. Remember, Dad? I told you he was doing the rank advancement camp this week, too. I didn't know it was going to be such a big deal." I'd lied about Hector in the note, but what I was saying now was all true. I was thinking about going to the library; I just didn't end up there.

Mom and Dad came and sat on either side of me. "Yes, I re-member now," said Dad. "But Sandy, we don't know anything about this kid or where he lives or who his parents are. We didn't even know where to start looking for you."

"We called Troy and Cassie and Shanika," Mom added, "But no one knew where you were. Shanika said that she brought you home after taekwondo, but she had no idea you and Hector were going to the library or which library you were going to."

It really bothered me that my parents had called Shanika. It sounded like she'd covered for me okay, but I'm pretty sure Shani-ka knew I wasn't at the library with Hector. And Troy. And Cassie. Who knew where they were or what they were doing.

I couldn't bring myself to ask about Cassie, but I really won-dered whether maybe Troy at least still cared a little. "Where was Troy?" I asked.

"At his uncle's garage working on a car," Mom answered. "He said that he'd been working all week and hadn't really even talked to you."

"Apparently, you haven't been talking to Cassie lately, either," Dad said.

"I've been at taekwondo camp all week!" The words came out a little more forcefully than I intended.

"We know that, Sandy. You don't have to get all defensive," said Mom.

"We're just worried, Sandy," Dad said with a sigh. "We're trying to figure out what's going on with you, and you're not giving us much to go on."

"What is it about taekwondo that has you so worried anyway?" I asked. I was starting to feel a little trapped between them and needed to orchestrate a graceful exit.

"It's not the taekwondo," said Dad. "We're actually very impressed with Mr. Washington and think that having a sport like that will look good on your college application."

Mom put her hand on my knee. "But Shanika is several years older than you are, and sometimes once the seniors have been admitted to a college, they start to slack off . . . " Mom let her voice trail off.

Dad completed her thought. "And party more."

Mom looked at Dad and then back to me. "Sandy, we've been wondering if the Nyquil was the only thing you've taken."

My face immediately flushed. Anger catapulted me from the couch. "I get it now," I said, turning to face my parents. "You think I'm out partying with Shanika because she's a senior or doing drugs with Hector because he's Hispanic! I don't believe you guys!"

My parents looked genuinely shocked. Mom recovered first. "Sandy, that's not what we were trying to say."

"That's what you think, though, isn't it?" I said it an accusatory tone I'd never used with my parents before. "Well, you're wrong. You really don't understand anything, do you?" And with that I stormed out of the living room and back into my room.

If I'd been going for drama and the full effect, I would have slammed my bedroom door, too, but I'd actually surprised myself. My heart was pounding, and I felt so overcome by adrenaline that I really think I could have pulled the door right off its hinges. I sat down on my bed and tried to sort through everything that had just happened. I had vodka in my backpack under my bed and another bottle hidden in my closet, but I didn't dare reach for it. I was pretty sure my parents would be knocking on my door any second.

I was trembling, but not because I wanted a drink. I suddenly felt so powerful—bigger than life. The anger was almost more intoxicating than the alcohol. *And guess what! I seem to have tapped in to an unlimited supply. It's all mine, it's free, and it's LEGAL!*

I could hear my parents still arguing with each other. I know I should have felt bad about that, but I was just glad they were leaving me alone. I picked up my notebook and pen and started thinking about how good it felt to be angry. *If jealousy is a green-eyed monster, maybe anger is a red-eyed monster.* But Shakespeare never wrote that. *Maybe I will* . . . So I sat on my bed and wrote this poem:

My Red-Eyed Monster

Such a bitter seed I swallowed.
No one saw, and no one knew.
I buried it inside myself

Where it took root and grew.

I felt it pierce my spirit
And worm into my veins.
It snaked my heart and arteries
And bound my soul in chains.

For weeks I've fed this monster
Stolen spirits laced with pain.
Still it slithers through me,
Deftly preying on my brain.

I feel it now in every cell.
My body's not my own.
And even though it's steeped in fear,
There's strength I've never known.

My timeless gladiator
Transcends gender, race and age.
From you, my red-eyed monster,
I accept this gift of RAGE.

I flipped back through the notebook and reread all the poems I'd written this past week. By this time, it was after 11:00, so I knew my parents weren't coming in to see me tonight. I thought about taking a drink, but then decided to relish a bit in my rage. I stood up and performed my white-belt form with more energy and precision than I'd ever imagined.

I am strong. I am powerful. I felt like I could master everything and everyone. So I ignored Mr. Conaway's voice in the back of my head whispering, *"But do you have character? Do you even know what character is?"*

Once I was certain my parents had gone to bed, I went downstairs and raided the refrigerator. For the first time in forever, I was hungry.

19

Write till your ink be dry, and with your tears,
Moist it again, and frame some feeling line
That may discover such integrity.

—*Two Gentlemen of Verona*, Act III, Scene ii, Lines 75-77

WHEN I CAME down for breakfast the next morning, we all just kind of pretended that last night never happened. I was sitting at the table, leaning over my cereal bowl and shoveling it in to make sure my mouth was full at all times. It was one of those April days where it rained nonstop, so when Dad offered to drive me to the library, the idea wasn't very appealing.

"I think I'll just work on the paper in my room," I said without bothering to swallow or sit up straight.

Mom came over and sat next to me drinking a cup of coffee. "So, only two more weeks until the school musical."

I nodded and kept shoveling. I wasn't going to encourage polite conversation on any topic. I wasn't really trying to be rude, but I could still feel the anger bubbling up under the surface of every word I spoke.

"We were able to get a Wednesday evening appointment with Dr. McMann at 7 p.m. so you won't have to miss rehearsal." Mom was staring at me expectantly. I just kept shoveling and chewing. Every now and then I made this slurping noise without really meaning to.

My father was sitting back away from the table, half hiding behind the morning paper. Occasionally he would glance at me like he was waiting for an apology or something. Or maybe he was debating whether he and Mom should apologize to me. *Ha! Not likely. But if he does, I think I'll tell him maybe he and Mom should go talk to Dr. McMann and leave me alone.*

When there was nothing left in my bowl to slurp or shovel, I mumbled, "May I be excused?" I didn't wait for a response; I just put my breakfast bowl and spoon in the dishwasher and retreated to my room.

I ran all the way through white belt form twice to release all the breakfast scene stress. I studied orange belt form a little bit, but then started thinking about my character assignment again. I was thinking that the poem I wrote on character might be okay to turn in, but after reading through it silently and then out loud I wasn't so sure. It sounded good to me, but was it really any good? *It's not Shakespeare, that's for sure. Shakespeare would write sonnets.*

That's when I remembered one of my favorite lines from *A Wrinkle in Time* where Mrs. Whatsit is talking about writing sonnets: "You're given the form, but you have to write the sonnet yourself. What you say is completely up to you." It seemed like a good way to approach this formless writing assignment . . . first define the form I want to use, give myself some boundaries, and then express myself through the form. *Maybe it will be liberating in the same way the taekwondo forms seem to be.*

Shakespeare wrote 154 sonnets. I had them all right there to-gether taking up less than 30 pages of my *Complete Works* volume. The form was pretty simple. Each poem had 14 lines, the first 12 divided into three stanzas and then a final couplet. It was all in iambic pentameter, which meant each line sounded like ta-DA ta-DA ta-DA ta-DA ta-DA. The first and third lines of each stanza rhymed and so did the second and fourth lines, then the last two lines in the couplet rhymed, too. The idea was to set out an issue or a problem in the first 12 lines and then summarize or resolve it in the last two. So I sat down and read all of Shakespeare's sonnets just to get the rhyme and rhythm pattern burned into my brain.

A lot of them were about love, like *Sonnet 18*, which starts out:

Shall I compare thee to a summer's day?
Thou art more lovely and more temperate.

I mostly ignored all of the gushy love stuff and read it all for meter. Like this:

Shall I comPARE thee TO a SUMmer's DAY? Thou ART more LOVEly AND more TEMperATE. But there were some with great one-liners tucked away in them. Like the final couplet in *Sonnet 28*:

But day doth daily draw my sorrows longer,
And night doth nightly make grief's strength seem stronger.

I was thinking a lot about what Mr. Washington had said. *A man's reputation is what other people think of him; his character is what he really is.* And just like that it came to me: *My character is who I really am.* Perfect iambic pentameter! All I needed was a rhyme for "am" and I had my final couplet. *My reputation's nothing but a sham.* Bingo! It helped to just sit and read one sonnet right after the other because my mind really was stuck in the meter.

I was on a roll when Mom knocked on the door. "Sandy?" she called softly as she knocked.

"Yeah?" I answered coolly.

"Do you mind if I come in?"

"You and Dad own the whole house, don't you?" I was surprised how quickly the monster could surface when I was feeling pretty good just a moment before.

I could hear Mom take a deep breath, weighing her words carefully. *Why is it suddenly so easy to be mean to her?*

"I just wanted to let you know that lunch is ready, if you'd like to join us."

Wow. Lunchtime already? Come to think of it, I am feeling hungry again.

"Okay," I said. This time I tried to sound a little nicer. "I'll be right down."

Nobody was saying much during lunch. Any other time I'd have been wondering who died. But I knew. It was my red-eyed monster that was controlling the room. Part of me felt a little bad for my parents because they really didn't deserve to be treated like this, but it just felt so good to be in control for a while. Still, Mom had broiled tuna steaks with ginger dressing and made California rolls, both of which she knew I absolutely loved. I decided to tell them about my progress to make them feel better.

"I've been working really hard on this assignment for World History," I said. You could almost hear the pressure whoosh out of my parents like when an 18-wheeler releases the engine break.

"What's the assignment?" Dad asked. He mixed some wasabi and soy sauce in a little dish.

"We're supposed to pick a question from a long list and answer it. I picked 'What is character?'" I motioned for him to pass me the soy sauce.

"That's a pretty big question," Mom jumped in. "You could write on that for years and still not get it exactly right."

Dad nodded. "No wonder you've been holed up in your room all morning. How long does it have to be?" He dipped a big piece of the roll in the mix using his chop sticks and stuffed it into his mouth. *So not pretty. That's why I use a fork and cut them in half.*

I shook off the urge to take a cheap shot at Dad while his mouth was full. "That's the thing," I replied. "There's no length requirement. It can be as long or as short as you want it to be. Longer is clearly not better, and anything that sounds 'canned' to Conaway is a total killer."

"I bet that set off a couple of your Type A classmates." Dad laughed.

I nodded. "Amy Taylor went berserk. Conaway suggested she choose the question 'What is Fair?'"

Mom smiled. "So where does one even begin with such an as- signment?"

I allowed myself a devilish grin. "Well, I'm glad you asked. All this taekwondo has me genuinely appreciating forms, so I asked myself what form Shakespeare would use if he were writing on character, and I decided to write a sonnet." I squeezed my lemon wedge over my tuna steak.

Dad beamed. "That's a great idea! So how's it coming?"

I was almost ready to spout off my final couplet, when I sud- denly realized I didn't want my parents to read my sonnet. I didn't want them to know my reputation is a sham. *What was I thinking! Why did I go and tell them I'm writing a sonnet?* My monster turned on me, and all I could do was shake my head. "Nothing yet. Maybe I'm not a poet after all." I cut a huge slice of tuna and forced it into my mouth. The monster was squeezing my throat so I really had to struggle to chew and swallow.

Dad didn't seem to notice. "I've got a great book on writing sonnets. I'll find it for you after lunch."

"Your father used to write me sonnets," Mom said reaching across the table and taking his hand. "Back in the day."

"You're still an inspiration," Dad said kissing her hand. "Maybe it's time I wrote you another sonnet. Get all of the creative juices in the household flowing."

Looks like they're through fighting. Maybe if they spend the rest of the weekend making up, they'll still leave me alone. I quickly scooped the rest of my California roll into my mouth. I soon as I could swallow, I asked to be excused.

"Don't you want some fresh fruit salad?" Mom asked.

"Maybe later. Right now I just want to get back to work."

"What about the book on sonnets?" Dad asked.

"I'll let you know if I need it," I replied.

20

If my slight Muse do please these curious days,
The pain be mine, but thine shall be the praise.

—*Sonnet 38*, Lines 13-14

I SURVIVED THE weekend and emerged from my cave with two sonnets. I couldn't decide which one I wanted to turn in, so I rewrote them both neatly in the back of my spiral notebook. I was leaning toward this one:

<u>*What Is Character?*</u>

Frustration seems to dominate my day.
Depression is my battle every night.
I choose to act like everything's okay.
I want the world to think that I'm alright.

Will Shakespeare says that "All the world's a stage."
But who creates the roles we choose to play?
I feel like I've been living in a cage
Designed to keep my demons all at bay.

Can anyone rewrite the script in hand?
My life's become a senseless tragedy.
But maybe I can choose to take a stand.
Forget about what others think of me.

My reputation's nothing but a sham.
My character is who I really am.

This seemed the safer of the two sonnets. My monster liked the other one best, just because it had the word "hell" in it, I think. Conaway is still pretty new and cool enough that he probably wouldn't make a big deal about that used in the proper context. And I had it in the proper context.

Behind the Mask

Behind the mask I choose to wear each day,
I hide all my confusion and my pain.
But hiding doesn't make it go away.
It only packs explosives in my brain.

I feel like I have swallowed a black hole.
The cold and empty darkness never ends.
Emotions trample down my weary soul,
No longer trusting any of my friends.

Forget it! Just forget it! But I can't . . .
The more I push it down the more I feel
I'm always walking slightly at a slant.
I have to figure out what's really real.

119

Each day that I decide I will not tell
Is one step farther down my road to hell.

I definitely didn't want my parents reading either of them. *What about McMann? Erin TheRapist? Are you going to let her read them?* The monster's voice again. I could feel my monster's predilection for danger—wanting to get me into trouble just for laughs. *I'm going to have to keep a close watch on the beast.*

I told my parents I was no Shakespeare when it came to writing sonnets and that I had to settle for a regular poem. I let them read the first *My Character* poem I wrote last weekend. That sounded more like the general teenage angst they expected me to have to deal with. Dad seemed a little disappointed, but Mom pulled him back. She told me that it was really lovely, and she was very proud of me. The monster was having a heyday taunting me with that, and it was all I could do to keep the tears in check without lashing out.

Dad drove me to school. I think he really wanted to help me turn my poem into a sonnet, and it was all he could do to leave it be. He talked a little about the musical, but mostly we rode in silence. I was trying to think of a way to get out of my appointment with Dr. McMann. I could hear the monster's sinister laugh in my mind. *Only two days until your date with Erin TheRapist. Better let me handle that.*

By the time I walked into the school, I was as tight as an overstretched violin string—sensitive to every vibration and ready to snap. I coasted through my morning classes and sat by myself at lunch. There was an empty chair between Cassie and Troy, but they never even looked at me. *Not like they're saving it for you. They're just growing apart, too.*

I was picking at my food when a hand on my shoulder startled me. "Hey, Sandy." It was Hector. "Mind if I sit down?"

"Go right ahead." I motioned to the seat next to me. "Congratulations on earning your yellow belt."

Hector turned the chair around and straddled it so he could lean over the back of the chair and still face me.

"Thanks," he said. "Your white form looked good, too."

We talked about Shanika and taekwondo and how it was too bad that seniors and sophomores had different lunch periods.

"So will I see you at the do-jahng tonight?" Hector asked me.

"Probably not," I replied. "I've got play practice."

"Oh, yeah. I heard you're Peter Pan."

I nodded. "I doubt I'll be there regularly until after the musical. Maybe Saturday morning, though."

"Shanika is in that, too, isn't she?" Hector asked.

I nodded. "She's Tiger Lily. You should see her dance."

Hector laughed. "I plan to. I want to get me a ticket right up front." Then he leaned closer to me and said in a sly whisper, "Don't tell Shanika I said so, but when she's not wearing those taekwondo pajamas, she is one hot *mamacita*." He exhaled heavily with a low whistle under his breath.

Figures! Hector's hot for Shanika. I tried to remember the expression on Shanika's face when she was telling me about what happened to Hector, but I don't think it was anything at all like the expression on Hector's face. *I wonder if he knows she knows all about the wrestling thing. Probably not. And he definitely doesn't know I know.* I felt a little guilty about how glad I was that I knew more about Hector than he knew about me.

Just then the bell rang. Hector was up and off in a single motion. "*Hasta luego,* Sandy."

I gave him a feeble wave. "See ya."

In World History, Conaway collected our assignments first thing. I was all ready to hand in just my *What Is Character?* sonnet, but at the very last second pulled out my notebook, ripped out my *Behind the Mask* sonnet and went up to Conaway's desk to staple them both together. It was a pretty lively class discussion with most people talking more about how much or how little they wrote and doing everything possible to avoid telling what they actually wrote.

Hamilton gave me a pass out of study hall last period to work on the musical. Shanika was there, too, so we went through all of our lines and songs together. Neither of us said anything about my parents calling her until after rehearsal was completely over. "Do you want a ride home?" she asked.

"Sure," I said. "Thanks. Just let me call my dad so he knows where I am." I started following her out to her car.

"That's a good idea," she said. "They seemed pretty worried about that Friday night." We both climbed in and buckled up.

"Yeah, I'm sorry about that—their giving you a call and everything," I said as I started dialing.

"Dad said he found you sleeping on the table behind the studio."

I winced. Fortunately, my dad picked up. "Hey, Dad. Shanika's taking me home, okay? Right now . . . No problem." I hung up.

"Everything cool?" Shanika asked, starting the engine.

"Yeah, he just wants to make sure I go right home and stay there." I was tempted to look out the window, but gathered my courage and turned to face Shanika instead.

"I'll take your butt right home all right, but are you gonna stay there?"

I nodded. "I'm on a new mission to stay OUT of trouble."

Shanika laughed. "All right, then. What was that chickenfeed story about you and Hector going to the library all about, anyway?"

"I just wanted to walk, and I thought my parents wouldn't worry if they thought I was at the library with Hector."

"Well, your mom sure sounded worried to me." Shanika rolled down her window. "We gotta let some of that fresh April air in here. Roll down your window, Sandy. A little breeze'll do you good."

We rode for a few minutes in silence. "So what's the deal with you and Hector now?"

I chuckled. "No deal. We're just friends because we both spent last week at camp." I studied Shanika's face. She was smiling. "So what's the deal with you and Hector? You know he's got a thing for you."

Shanika let out a shrill screech. "For me? You think something's going on between me and Hector?"

"I'm just sayin'," I nodded. "He thinks you're one hot *mamacita.*"

"Shut up!" Shanika howled. "Did he actually say that?"

"He did." We were pulling up to my house now, so I pulled my backpack up from between my feet onto my lap. "Only don't tell him I told you, or he'll never talk to me again."

"Oh, I won't tell. I promise!" Shanika pulled into my drive and put the car in park. "Cross my heart I won't tell. What else did he say?"

"Nothing," I replied. "Just that he's planning to come and see you in the musical."

Shanika just sat there for a moment, smiling and bobbing her head. "That's cool," she said. "Maybe we can fill a whole section with taekwondo ninjas!"

"You're probably the first Tiger Lily with a black belt in martial arts," I said getting out of the car.

"Not just a blackbelt, Sandy," Shanika called to me through the window. "Third degree blackbelt! Don't forget the third degree part!"

21

Let it suffice thee that I trust thee not.

—*As You Like It*, Act I, Scene iii, Line 57

IT WASN'T UNTIL I started unpacking my backpack at home that evening that I realized my spiral notebook was missing. *I took it to school. I know I took it to school because I had both of my sonnets in it for World History.* At first I thought someone had stolen it, but then as I retraced my steps in my mind, I realized I must have left it on Conaway's desk when I stapled my two sonnets together.

I collapsed on my bed in a full-blown panic attack. My heart pounded as I gasped for breath. *This cannot be happening.* I tried to calm myself down and think about what this really meant. Conaway had the two sonnets I turned in for my assignments. *He might not even open the notebook. He might not read anything. He might just give it back to me tomorrow. No problem.* No problem—except I knew he would have to open the notebook to see whose it was. And the only way he'd know who it belonged to would be by finding the rough drafts of my sonnets inside.

Screwed. I am so totally screwed. But I wasn't sure what Conaway would do. I went into my closet and pulled out the vodka. I hadn't had a drink in days. I was a little afraid that Dr. McMann might test me for alcohol, and I wanted to be totally clean. I put the bottle on the dresser in front of me and started doing my white belt form. *Step and high-block. Focus. Punch.* By the time I finished I was ready to hide the vodka back in my closet. And I did it without taking a drink.

I sat back down on the bed and started reading through all of my Peter Pan lines. I'd been a little rusty in spots at rehearsal. Mom had a dinner meeting, so it was just Dad and me for dinner. I talked him into eating in the living room and watching *Hamlet* with me. Cassie and Troy had given it to me on my birthday, but it was still wrapped in the original cellophane. We were still watching it when Mom got home. It felt good to lose myself so totally for several hours.

The moment I went to bed all of my worries returned. I didn't feel so panicky, though. I just lay awake most of the night wondering what Conaway would do and whether there was any way to get through all of this without having everything explode in my face. My parents still didn't know about the grocery store incident. With each passing day, it seemed less likely that the store would call my parents. *Maybe if you just stay away like they told you, the whole thing will blow over. It's either going to blow over or blow up.*

And then there was Shanika's wanting me to tell somebody about Aaron. *How about Erin TheRapist? Do you want to tell Erin TheRapist about Aaron the rapist? Why? Why should I tell? What good would it do now?*

I woke up the next morning thinking maybe Conaway hadn't even noticed the notebook on his desk, or at least hadn't done anything with it. So I got to school a little early and went directly to his classroom. He was sitting behind his desk grading papers.

"Mr. Conaway?" My voice quavered as I said it.

He looked up. "Good morning, Sandy."

I walked toward the desk. "Good morning."

"I was hoping I might have a chance to talk with you today. Have a seat. I'm glad you stopped by."

I sat down at the desk closest to his. My eyes searched his desktop, but there was no sign of my notebook. "I was wondering if I left my notebook in your classroom yesterday," I stammered.

Mr. Conaway opened the drawer on his right and pulled out my notebook. "Here it is," he said handing it to me. He waited to see if I was going to say anything more, but I was too busy stuffing the notebook as deep as possible down into my backpack.

"Sandy, I read the poems you turned in on character. They're very good."

"So I get an 'A'?" I asked bitterly. I could feel the monster wanting to come out to play with Conaway.

"As a matter of fact, you do," he replied slowly. "But I'm really worried about you and want to make sure you're okay."

"I'm fine," I said smoothly. "Just a little bit of creative writing. Isn't that what you wanted?"

"Your poetry has a 'raw truth' feeling to it." He waited, but I didn't respond. "And then there's the notebook. I had to see what was in it to know whose it was."

"So now you know." I stood up to leave. "Thanks."

Mr. Conaway stood up, too. "Sandy, wait. I want you to know that I talked to the guidance counselor about your poems . . . and the notebook."

My heart dropped to the pit of my stomach. I shook my head and turned to walk away. Mr. Conaway came around his desk to where I was and placed himself strategically between me and the

127

doorway. "I think maybe it would be a good idea for you to talk to the counselor, too."

"Yeah, well, I really appreciate your concern and all, but I already have an appointment with a Dr. McMann tomorrow evening, so I think I'd just as soon save it for her."

As soon as the words "Dr. McMann" passed my lips, Conaway looked relieved. *There you go. Not your problem anymore. You can wash your hands of the whole mess.*

Conaway's face brightened. "Dr. McMann," he repeated nodding. "That's good. I'm really glad to hear that."

"So is it okay if I go now? I don't want to be late to my first period class."

Conaway moved to the side to let me pass. "Oh, sure," he said motioning me on by with his hands. "I'll just see you this afternoon in class."

And so the crisis passed. The rest of the day was completely uneventful. At least, it was until I got home. Shanika drove me home after rehearsal. As we approached my house, we saw a police car sitting in the driveway.

22

Truth is truth.
To the end of reckoning.

—*Measure for Measure*, Act V, Scene i, Lines 45-46

I PANICKED AT the thought of the police already talking to my parents. Shanika drove past without slowing down. She drove several more blocks and found a safe place to pull over. I jumped out of the car and started pacing.

Shanika turned the car off, stepped out and slammed the car door behind her. "What do you want to do, Sandy?" Shanika finally asked me.

"What should I do?" I asked.

"Well, you're going to have to go home eventually." She walked around to the back of the car and propped herself up against the trunk.

"Maybe I can just wait until after the police leave," I suggested.

Shanika nodded. "Check your phone," she instructed. "See if you have a message from your parents.

I went back into the car, pulled out my phone, and checked for messages. "Nothing," I said.

"Maybe you should call them and see what they say."

I shoved the phone in my jacket pocket and tried to figure out what to do. I leaned over the car with both palms of my hands on top of the trunk and tried to breathe. "They'll tell me to come home," I concluded. Just then my phone rang.

"Are you going to answer it?" Shanika asked.

I took a deep breath and nodded. The caller ID flashed Home. "Hello," I answered tentatively.

"Hi, Sandy. It's me, Dad. Where are you?"

"Shanika's bringing me home. But we were wondering if it would be okay for me to go with her to pick up a pizza and take it back to her dad at the studio."

"Not tonight, Sandy. I want you to come straight home."

I knew it wasn't worth arguing, but wanted to see what he might tell me. "Why? What's up?" I could see Shanika straining to hear what Dad would say. I held the phone several inches away from my ear so she could hear, too.

"Nothing's up. I just want you to come straight home. Where are you now?"

"In Shanika's car." I answered. "I'll be home soon."

As I hung up the phone, Shanika exclaimed, "Nothing's up! How do you like that?" We both got back into the car. "He knows you're going to see the police car as soon as you get there."

I took a deep breath. "I don't care," I said. "I really don't."

Shanika gave me a weird look, but then asked, "What do you want me to do?"

"Just drive me home."

Shanika turned the car around and started driving back toward my house. "Do you want me to go in with you?"

YES! I wanted to scream. Instead I looked away. "This is my mess. I guess it's time I faced it." I looked back at Shanika and felt tears forming in the corners of my eyes. "Thanks, though." I wiped my eyes.

Neither of us said another word until I was getting out of the car to go inside. "Sandy," Shanika said. "Call me and let me know what happens, okay?"

I nodded.

When I walked in, Mom and Dad and two uniform police officers were all sitting around the kitchen table. Mom had a legal pad she was scratching notes on. Dad had a glass of wine and was flipping through some papers. Mom rushed to greet me, gave me a big hug and whispered in my ear, "I don't want you to say anything until we figure out what's going on."

She introduced me to the officers and then said, "If you'll excuse us, my husband and I would like to talk to Sandy privately for a moment." She motioned to Dad to come with us. "If you want to wait right here, we'll be in the study."

As we walked into the back room, I felt my pulse quickening, and the monster taking over. "Nothing's up!" I shouted at Dad. "You're sitting here talking to the police and nothing's up!"

"Lower your voice, Sandy," my mom instructed. "You haven't been exactly forthcoming with us lately either."

Touché. I shut my mouth, seething in the silence. I waited for my parents to sit down, but they didn't. *Apparently we're not staying long.*

"For God's sake, Sandy," Dad said. "Just help us understand what happened."

"Nothing," I retorted. "The store thought I was shoplifting and banned me from ever going back. End of story."

My parents looked fully taken aback. "Shoplifting?" Mom asked. "You think this is about shoplifting?"

"What store are you talking about?" Dad demanded.

Mom waved her hands. "We can talk about that after the police leave." She reached out her hand toward Dad. "Here, give me the notebook copies."

As Dad passed the papers to Mom, I could see that the notebook that had been copied was mine . . . the one I left in Conaway's class. I gasped and tried to grab the papers from my Mom. She handed them to me without a struggle.

"Maybe we'd better sit down," Mom said. We sat on the leather couch, Mom and Dad on opposite ends and me in the middle. "Sandy, the officers are here to investigate a possible sexual assault."

I dropped the papers, balled my hands up in fists and pressed the heels of my palms as hard as I could into my eyes to hold back the tears. It was no use. I wept uncontrollably. My parents enveloped me in their arms and let me cry. Eventually, I struggled to free myself and motioned toward the box of Kleenex. Dad got them for me. Still, my throat was swollen shut and my nose so stuffed up that I couldn't speak.

"Can you tell us what happened?" Mom asked softly.

I picked up the papers, handed them to her and threw my hands up in the air as if to say, "It's all there." I was breathing so heavily. Every time I tried to say a word, all that escaped was a high-pitched whine. I blew my nose and shook my head and blew my nose again.

After several totally "mom" moments, Mom shifted into her lawyer mode. "Here's what we're going to do," she said turning to my dad. "These officers just need to make an initial report. They need enough details to determine a crime occurred and have a detective assigned to the case. That detective is going to want to talk to Sandy. It's not going to happen tonight." Mom turned back to me. "Okay, Sandy?"

I nodded. She put one hand on my knee and lifted my chin up with her other hand so she could look me in the eyes. "You're not going to talk to the police tonight. But I need to you answer a few simple questions for me right now."

I nodded.

"Were you sexually assaulted?"

Tears filled my eyes as I broke down again. My parents encircled me once more.

"I need you to at least nod or shake your head," Mom continued gently. "Can you do that?"

I nodded.

So Mom asked me again, "Were you sexually assaulted?"

I nodded. I began to feel Dad shaking beside me, but he didn't let me go, and he didn't say a word.

"Was it Aaron Jackson?" Mom asked.

I nodded. Dad held me tighter.

"Cassie's boyfriend?" he asked.

I nodded again. Mom took a deep breath and reached for a Kleenex for herself. Then she handed one to Dad. They were both crying now, too.

"The officers are going to need to know where you were when it happened," Mom said softly.

"At Cassie's." It sounded more like a long whimper than actual words.

"At Cassie's?" Mom confirmed.

I nodded.

"Okay, Sandy, just one more question and then I'll go back and talk to the police." She sighed deeply. "Do you remember when it happened?"

I nodded. "The Ides of March," I mumbled.

"Sometime in March?" asked Mom.

"The Ides of March," said Dad. "March 15."

I nodded.

Mom gave me a big hug. "I'll be right back," she said. "You two stay here."

Dad and I waited in silence. I leaned back on the couch, closed my eyes and let myself drift off to Neverland. I could hear Wendy's voice: *You just think happy thoughts. They just lift you in the air.* But no happy thoughts came. So I tried to think of nothing instead.

When Mom came back, she told us the officers wanted to take my notebook with them. I pulled it out of my backpack for her. She quickly compared it to the photocopied pages. "Have you written anything new today?" she asked.

I shook my head.

"All right, then. I'm going to let them have the notebook, and we'll keep the copy."

23

How poor are they that have not patience!
What wound did ever heal but by degrees?

—*Othello*, Act II, Scene iii, Lines 376-377

I DIDN'T GO to school the next day. Dad stayed with me in the morning; then Mom came home for the afternoon when Dad had classes to teach. We were all together for lunch, though, and that's when we started really talking again. I told them about the drinking, and the alcohol I'd taken from their liquor cabinet and the stores. I assured them I was done with drinking, but I didn't tell them about the vodka I still had hidden in my closet. *Just a little extra security, just in case.*

I didn't tell them that I was with Aaron and Cassie when I took that first drink, either. When Dad brought the subject of Aaron up, Mom told me that I could talk about it if I wanted, or that I could wait until our appointment with Dr. McMann that evening. Then we talked about the whole Erin/Aaron and therapist/theRapist thing and whether I thought I could be comfortable talking to Dr. McMann.

"I'll cancel the appointment if you want me to," my mom said. "But all three of us need to get in to see a therapist as soon as possible."

"You mean a *counselor*, right?" Dad interjected.

"Sorry," Mom apologized. "I plan to remove the word therapist completely from my vocabulary."

"Let's just see how it goes tonight," I said.

The phone rang as we were eating and talking, but no one rose to answer it. "If it's important, they'll leave a message," Dad said. It was, and they did. A Detective Morales left the message saying she wanted to arrange a time to talk with me. "Can we wait until after we meet with Dr. McMann?" Dad asked Mom.

"I don't see why not," Mom agreed. "I'll return the call tomorrow morning."

"Just make sure it doesn't interfere with rehearsals," I said. I was already stressing about having to miss rehearsal that afternoon since I wasn't at school. So I watched the old *Peter Pan* video starring Mary Martin and studied my lines all afternoon.

When it was finally time to go to our appointment with the counselor, Mom grabbed her keys and called for Dad to come out of the study.

"Can I drive?" I asked. I'd had my permit since driver's training last summer, but we'd agreed to wait until summer to get me my license and a car. "I need the practice driving downtown, and it's past rush hour."

Mom exchanged a glance with Dad before nodding. "Here you go," she said, handing me the keys. "And your dad can ride up front with you. I'll be happy to take a back seat this evening."

We rode in silence. My parents firmly believed music or conversation was an unnecessary distraction for teenage drivers. So I pushed everything else from my mind and focused on driving my mom's Mercedes. It wasn't new or fancy, but I loved the Metallic Steel Grey color and how powerful it felt to be in the driver's seat with my hands on the steering wheel.

There was nobody in the waiting area when we arrived at Erin TheRapist's office. Dad and I sat down in chairs on either side of a table with magazines, and Mom went up to ring the bell by the abandoned receptionist desk. Erin TheRapist appeared within seconds.

Mom handled the introductions, then Erin TheRapist suggested that she meet with each of us briefly, individually during the first part of our session, and then together during the last half. She turned to me and smiled brightly, 'Would you like to go first, last or in between?"

Or how about not at all? I shrugged. Everyone was staring at me, waiting for me to answer. "Why do I have to decide?" I asked finally.

"You don't have to if you don't want to." Her voice was reassuring. "Who would you like to decide?"

I shook my head, trying to figure out the game she seemed to be playing. Suddenly I wanted to talk to Mom. "Dad can go first," I said.

Erin TheRapist nodded. "Dr. Peareson, if you'll follow me, please."

"Certainly," Dad said, "And you can call me Bill."

Mom sat down in the chair beside me. I picked up a *People* magazine and started leafing through it. Mom pulled her reading glasses and an advance sheet of recent court decisions from her bag. I watched her as she started reading.

"So how much have you already told her?" I asked.

Mom removed the reading glasses from her nose before turning to look me in the eyes. "Pretty much everything I know about what's been going on."

I rolled up the magazine and used it to tap on the table like a drumstick. "Has she seen the notebook?"

Mom nodded. "I faxed her the pages last night after you went to bed."

I swallowed hard and tried to look like it didn't matter. "Did you know she was going to meet with us individually at first?"

"No." Mom shook her head. "This was scheduled as a family session, so I just assumed we'd all go in together." She pulled a pint-size water bottle from her bag and held it out towards me. "Want a drink of water?"

I shook my head and unrolled the magazine like I was going to read again.

Mom opened the bottle and took a drink. "Let me know if you want some. I've got another one."

I stared at the bag and wondered what all it contained. Mom stuff. Lawyer stuff. Woman stuff. All the stuff we might need. I rolled the magazine up in the opposite direction to straighten it back out again. "So why do you think she's doing it?" I asked. "To divide and conquer?"

Mom looked at me and smiled. "Maybe," she answered, raising her eyebrows. "Or maybe she just wants the chance to establish rapport with us individually or to see if there's anything we have on our minds that we might be reluctant to say in a family session."

"Do you think Dad has something to say that he doesn't want you to hear?" I asked.

Mom sighed. "I really don't know, Sandy. I don't know much of anything anymore."

"Do you want to go next?" I asked.

"Up to you."

We sat in silence. I wanted to go sit on her lap, like I used to when I was a kid, and have her wrap her arms around me and hold me tight until I felt nothing but safe and loved. She used to kiss me on my forehead and call me her beautiful child. *When was the last time? Third grade? Fourth grade?* By sixth grade I was as tall as she was. She'd still sneak up behind me sometimes, though, when I was sitting at the table and plant a big kiss on top of my head. *Nobody but my mom ever kisses me anymore.*

I opened the magazine back up and pretended to read.

"Who's next?" Erin TheRapist asked when she and Dad returned.

"Mom," I said without looking up. Mom packed up her reading and followed Erin TheRapist back into whatever waited behind that door. Dad took her seat next to me, but didn't say anything.

"So where did she take you?" I asked, wanting to hear every detail.

"Back to her office," Dad replied. He picked up a *Reader's Digest,* but didn't open it.

"What's it like back there?"

"Cozy. There's an overstuffed chair and a loveseat. No couch big enough for me to lie down on." Dad forced a phony smile.

"So what did you talk about?" I asked. I noticed that I was bouncing my right leg nervously, but I didn't feel like trying to stop it.

"We talked about me. What I want to happen in our family." I watched him closely as he spoke, trying to gauge whether he was holding back, whether they'd really just been talking about me. I waited to see if he would volunteer more, but he turned back to the

Reader's Digest. We waited in silence for Mom and Erin TheRapist to return.

When my turn came, Mom gave me a big hug before sending me back with Erin TheRapist. Her office was bigger than I had pictured. A built-in bookshelf covered the wall by the doorway. There was a desk in front of that with different colored files neatly stacked on one corner and journals stacked on another. Over by the window was the loveseat and chair Dad had described. There was also a table and two chairs off to the left of that.

"Have a seat wherever you'd like," offered Erin TheRapist. So I sat down in the chair behind her desk.

24

Yet this shall I ne'er know, but live in doubt
Till my bad angel fire my good one out.

—*Sonnet 144*, Lines 13-14

IF ERIN THE Rapist was surprised or upset that I was sitting behind her desk, she didn't show it. She went over and sat down on the love seat. "Thank you for agreeing to talk with me privately before we do a family session," she said.

I felt myself swiveling back and forth in her chair. I looked up and met her gaze, but I didn't say anything. In my mind I could hear the monster chanting *Aaron the Rapist, Erin TheRapist.* First the shout, *Aaron the Rapist!* Followed by an echo, *Erin TheRapist.* I looked away.

"Maybe we should start with your just telling me a little bit about yourself." She looked so relaxed, like this was some sort of college interview or something.

Psycho Therapy. Psycho Therapist. Tell her what she wants to hear.

"I was sexually assaulted." I blurted it out like I didn't even care, but I was swiveling faster now.

She nodded. "One time or more than one time?"

I stopped swiveling. "One time."

She nodded again. "How long ago was that?"

I stared at her. "March 15," I said. The words sounded cold and sent a shiver down my spine.

"Of this year?" she asked, oblivious to the coolness that suddenly permeated the room.

I nodded.

She leaned forward. Resting her elbows on her thighs, she clasped her hands together as if she were going to pray, but her eyes stayed focused right on me. "Sandy, we can talk about the sexual assault as much as you like, but that single event doesn't have to define you. I'd like you to tell me what you would have told me about yourself if I'd asked you on March 14th."

My monster fled. Tears filled my eyes and began spilling out, rolling down my cheeks. She reached for a box of Kleenex from the table and held it out toward me.

"It's okay, Sandy," she said.

I stood and slowly walked over to accept the box of Kleenex. Instead of taking it back behind the desk, I collapsed in the overstuffed chair beside her.

"On March 14th I would have told you that my life was perfect." I pulled a Kleenex from the box and blotted my eyes and nose. "I had the lead in the spring musical, plans to go to Juilliard, dreams of becoming a rising star on Broadway, maybe even in Hollywood."

"Do you still have the lead in the spring musical?" she asked quietly.

I nodded.

"Do you still want to go to Juilliard and become a big star?"

I shrugged, took a deep breath and blew my nose. "I don't know what I want anymore," I confessed.

She nodded. "That's okay, too." She sat up straight again. "Sandy, is there anything that you'd rather not talk about with your parents in the family session?"

I wadded up my used Kleenex and pulled a second one from the box. "I don't know."

"Normally, I would ask you to call me Erin," she began. I bristled at the name spoken aloud. "Under the circumstances, that doesn't seem like a good idea, but Dr. McMann sounds so formal. What would be most comfortable for you, Sandy?"

I wrapped the clean Kleenex around the dirty one and thought about this for a moment. She didn't try to push me or rush me. She just waited and gave me time to think. Finally, it came to me. "Can I just call you 'Doc?'" I asked.

She smiled warmly. "Sounds good to me."

"You don't think it sounds too much like a dwarf or Bugs Bunny or anything?" I could feel myself breathing more deeply.

She laughed. "I don't. And I much prefer 'Doc' over 'Grumpy' or 'Sneezy.'"

"Or I could call you Snow White," I offered.

"No, thank you!" She leaned back into the seat and shook her head. "The idea of waiting for a prince to come along and save me has never really appealed to me."

I gave her a soft chuckle without meaning to. "Then 'Doc' it is." I looked at the clock. Nearly 20 minutes had passed. "Anything else we need to talk about before we bring in Mom and Dad?"

Doc hesitated. "Maybe," she said. "Your parents want to talk about your meeting with a detective. Are you ready to talk about that?"

"I don't know, Doc," I replied. "Do I have to do the talking or can I just listen to what my parents want to say?"

"Tonight you can just listen, but that detective is going to want you to do the talking, in detail about what happened."

I nodded. "Do you think we could put that off until after the musical next week?"

"Maybe. We can talk about the best timing with your mom. If there's anyone who knows how to make the system work for you, it's your mom." She waited several moments. "Shall I go get your parents?"

I nodded. While she was gone I stood up, walked over to the wastebasket, and threw away my wadded up Kleenex. I scoped out the room again and decided to sit in the chair behind the table. I picked up one of Doc's journals and buried my nose in it.

I could feel my parents watching me when they came in the room, but I didn't look up. In my peripheral vision, I saw them sit down on the love seat—first Mom, then Dad. Doc sat in the over-stuffed chair. Dad cleared his throat, but didn't say anything. We all waited. I sneaked a peak at Doc. She seemed to be watching us patiently to see who was most uncomfortable with the silence.

That would be Dad. He broke the silence. "So are we ready to begin?"

Doc smiled at him and nodded. "You can start with whatever's on your mind, Bill."

Dad looked at me, then Mom and finally turned to Doc. "This is all so overwhelming to me. But I think what's been bothering me more than anything is the lying and the stealing. I just don't understand where that came from, and I want it to stop immediately."

Doc waited to be certain Dad was finished. "I think we're learning where Sandy's lying and stealing have come from, and as we

144

address the underlying issues, the symptoms will disappear. She turned to me. "Do you want to say anything about how you were getting the alcohol and the deception that's gone with it?"

I felt my eyes watering and just shrugged my shoulders. I tried to look at Dad directly, but I couldn't. I wasn't really ready to face him or Mom. I turned to Doc. "I'm sorry." Long pause. "I don't know what else I can say."

Doc nodded.

"It's like we've always said," Dad interjected. "Part of being truly sorry is not doing it anymore."

There was another long moment of silence. "How do you feel about that, Sandy?" Doc asked me.

I never really meant to lie to my parents and I hated the stealing. *At least he didn't say, "No more drinking."* I thought about the vodka in my closet. No more stealing was much easier than no more drinking. "No more stealing," I agreed. I felt like I was crossing my fingers behind my back, but I added, "And no more lying." *Maybe just not saying anything is close enough for now.*

Doc talked for most of the rest of the session. Mom and Dad agreed to put the detective off until after the musical. Mom would call and schedule the appointment tomorrow, though, just so they knew we were cooperating in the investigation.

Then Doc started defending me to my parents. "I don't condone breaking the law," she began, "but all things considered, Sandy has made some very positive choices in dealing with an incredibly stressful and difficult situation. The writing . . . the martial arts . . . Most kids would not have the resilience to distance themselves from friends who were not supportive and find new friends who were. Some kids never, ever find the courage to tell."

She paused, taking a good look at each one of us. "There's a lot for us to work on, but there's a lot for us to work with, too. Your family is strong. You're going to get through this."

She said it with such assurance, I almost believed her.

25

O Time thou must untangle this, not I!
It is too hard a knot for me to untie!

—*Twelfth Night*, Act II, Scene ii, Lines 38-39

SHANIKA TEXTED ME that night asking if everything was okay and wondering why I wasn't at school or rehearsal that day. I texted her back saying I was fine and that I'd catch up with her tomorrow. The next day she seemed surprised that the police were investigating the sexual assault rather than the shoplifting. But we were both happy to focus on the musical and leave everything else for afterwards.

As show time drew nearer, Shanika picked me up each morning and drove me home after rehearsals every evening. We were really clicking together on stage. The timing, the energy, everything just seemed to flow whenever we both took the stage. Hamilton even commented on it.

Friday night was opening night, and Saturday night was closing night with no performances to worry about in between. "Make 'em both count!" Hamilton advised. My parents and grandparents came to both. Shanika's dad came to both. I even saw Hector in the front row both nights. I didn't see Troy or Cassie either night.

Just as well. Cassie doesn't go anywhere without Aaron anymore. I'd had another session with Doc, and we talked about what I might do in case I ran into Aaron or he came to the musical. But he wasn't there, and I'd managed to avoid him entirely all week.

Both shows were a huge success with encores and curtain calls, flowers and accolades. During the cast party Saturday night I honestly felt like myself again, and it was totally cool hanging with Shanika all night. We were still laughing and talking a mile a minute on the drive to my house. Shanika's eyes shone when she looked at me, and for a moment all was right with the world. I was with Shanika who, on top of being a senior and blackbelt and all that, looked 100 percent regal tonight. In her shimmering purple blouse, still wearing most of her stage make-up, she could have been Queen Latifah's daughter.

I wished the night would never end, but before I knew it we were pulling into my driveway. As I went to get out of the car, Shanika punched my shoulder and said, "Ya done good, kid!"

"Thanks," I replied. But as I closed the car door behind me I realized she probably meant it. *I'm just a kid to her. She's a senior; I'm a sophomore. She's a black belt; I'm an orange belt. Now that the musical is over, taekwondo is the only place I'll ever see her.*

It was after midnight, but Mom was waiting up for me. "Did you have a good time?" she asked.

I nodded.

"That was another fine performance tonight," Mom said. "You and Shanika really stole the show!"

"I gotta crow!" I sang, spreading my arms out and adding a little dance move for effect.

"Your dad and I were very proud of you up there on stage," she added.

"Thanks, Mom." She came over and gave me a hug. "I think I'm ready to call it a night," I said.

"Me, too!" And with that she kissed my forehead, unleashed a huge, hippo yawn and wished me sweet dreams.

As I headed off to my room, my emotions plunged deeper toward despair with each physical step I climbed. *Now what?* I asked myself. The only thing I had to look forward to was talking to a detective. *And Shanika's graduation. It's all downhill from here,* I thought as I drifted off to sleep.

On Sunday, I spent most of the day in my room hoping Shanika would text me or call. She didn't. I practiced white belt form and one steps and worked on my new orange belt form.

I thought long and hard about the promises I'd made to my parents and Doc. *No more Nyquil. No more stealing. No more lying.* No one said anything about drinking. I had vodka, still hidden in my closet in case of an emergency. *Is this an emergency?* I asked myself. *Most definitely!* The voice of the monster mocked me. *It's a RE-emergency. Time for me to re-emerge!*

So that night, after my parents went to bed, I dug the vodka out of my closet and gulped several ounces. I lay back on my bed and waited for the red-eyed monster to take control. But the monster seemed to be playing hide-and-seek. I took another swig in search of the rage. I called for the monster the way Dad used to call for me as a kid. *All-ye all-ye "outs" in free!* Nothing. No anger. No rage. Nothing but a pile of emotional ashes. So I sat all alone in my room making mud pies out of my emotional ashes and firewater.

My red-eyed monster was gone. If any monster remained, it was a black-eyed monster of depression. Not black eyeballs . . . empty, eternal black holes in the hollows that should be eye sockets. I drank and devised elaborate plans to get more vodka without actually lying or stealing. I drank until the vodka was all gone and the room was spinning. I was the little ball in the roulette wheel bouncing back and forth between red and black spaces, feeling odd by trying to get even, wondering if my luck had finally completely run out.

Take me back to Never-Never Land. I don't want to face tomorrow. I don't want to face my parents. I don't want to talk to a detective. I would not allow myself to go to sleep, but I could not keep myself from passing out.

We were scheduled to meet with Detective Morales first thing Monday morning. She wasn't at all what I expected. For starters, despite her name, she definitely was not Hispanic. She had short blond hair and deep blue eyes, and she was dressed in full police uniform, including a bullet-proof vest, gun and Taser. She was all business. After a few formalities, she got right to the point. Yes, I wanted my parents in the room with me. No, I didn't object to having my statements recorded. Yes, I promised to tell the truth, the whole truth and nothing but the truth under the penalty of perjury.

"Now, Sandy," said Detective Morales, "I want you to tell me exactly what happened in your own words."

I went through the who, what, when and where. I had no real answers for why. I tried to just stick to the facts. Aaron did this. Aaron did that.

She had a hundred questions. She went back over everything, detail by detail, body part by body part. What did I do? Why did I do that? Why didn't I do this? Did anyone see? Why didn't I tell someone right away?

"I don't know," I kept saying. I looked at my parents. They were both glaring at the detective. My mom looked ready to pounce on her at any moment. She was gripping Dad's leg under the table, and he was pressing tightly down on her hand as if to hold her back.

Finally, we returned to a question I could answer. "Who is the first person you told?"

"Shanika Washington," I replied.

Detective Morales stopped. She looked hard at my mother and then turned back to me. "Is Shanika a female, black, age 18?"

I nodded. "She's a senior at West Side. We were in the musical together."

"I'll be right back." Detective Morales turned the recorder off, gathered all of her paperwork together and exited stage left. The door clanged loudly behind her.

Dad almost jumped from his chair. "That was awfully abrupt!" he exclaimed, turning to Mom. "What's going on?"

Mom looked troubled. "I wish I knew." Mom stood up, pushed in her chair, and began to pace slowly back and forth. "Did you see the look on her face when Sandy mentioned Shanika?"

"Whatever it is, it isn't good," said Dad.

Mom turned to me. "Sandy, has Shanika ever been in trouble that you know about?"

"No, Mom." I shook my head. "She's a black belt. Honesty, integrity, perseverance, and all that."

We waited in silence.

When Detective Morales returned she did not turn the recorder back on. "Mr. and Mrs. Peareson, there are two police reports that I think you should be aware of." She handed a copy to my mother and acted as if I no longer existed. "The most recent one is from just a few weeks ago where it was alleged that Sandy was stealing alcohol from a grocery store for one Shanika Washington, female/black/18."

"That's not true!" I pounded my fist on the table.

"Sandy!" Mom reprimanded me sternly. "You need to be quiet. Don't say another word until you and I have had a chance to speak privately." Mom read the report and then handed it to Dad. "What is the other report?"

Detective Morales was not so quick to hand this one over. "The other one is from two years ago. It's a report of rape made by one Shanika Washington, female/black/16 against one Aaron Jackson, male/white/16.

No! Shanika? Aaron? That can't be right. I felt like the frog we dissected in biology, hands and feet pinned spread-eagle, and a sharp little scalpel slicing me open from my throat down to the pit of my stomach.

"May I see that report?" Mom asked curtly.

"Be my guest," responded Detective Morales, handing over the second report.

We all waited while Mom read. When she looked up she said, "It looks like this was never even forwarded to the district attorney for prosecution."

"That's because it wasn't," agreed the detective. "There was no evidence of force. The general consensus was that Ms. Washington consented to the sexual relations, but then experienced 'buyer's remorse' afterward or, more probably, when her father found out that she was dating Mr. Jackson. Case closed."

26

"My salad days,
When I was green in judgment . . . "

—*Antony and Cleopatra,* Act I, Scene v, Lines 73-74

CASE CLOSED. DETECTIVE Morales' words rang in my ears. I felt the walls closing in around me. *Which case?* They wanted to blame Shanika for my shoplifting. I could barely bring myself to consider the other case. The detective and Mom were still talking, but their words were a senseless jumble. Their voices beat against my eardrum, but the sounds carried no meaning.

Shanika dated Aaron? Aaron raped Shanika? She never told me anything . . . Confusion choked me. I blinked my eyes and found myself staring hard at the spiral notebook sealed in a plastic evidence bag. *My notebook.* I reached for it.

Detective Morales snatched the bag away from my reach. "Oh, no you don't!" she barked. This catapulted my father to his feet, but instead of going for her or my notebook, he grabbed my shoulders and held me back.

I shrugged free from his grasp. "I want my notebook back."

Silence.

153

"Give me back my notebook," I demanded evenly.

"Sandy," Mom began, but Detective Morales interrupted her.

"It's evidence of an alleged crime," the detective growled.

"But it doesn't sound like you intend to investigate the real crime here." Mom was standing now. "Give Sandy the notebook, and we'll be on our way."

Detective Morales snarled, "You know I need permission from the D.A.'s office to do that." She looked most displeased as she shuffled her papers and my notebook back into a file folder.

"So you do intend to investigate the case and send it to the D.A. for prosecution?" Mom asked.

The detective scowled. "I may as well send it over right now. What else am I going to uncover in an investigation? It's been months since the incident. Sandy's already told me Cassie and Troy were there, and they didn't see anything. Sandy didn't even tell them anything. Sandy and Aaron are the only ones who know what really happened. Do you really think Aaron is going to corroborate Sandy's story?" She glared at Mom. "I mean, if he doesn't lawyer up, right, Mrs. Peareson?"

More silence. The air was rigged with infrared rays shooting back and forth between Detective Morales and my parents. Any motion, any sound could set off a nuclear explosion. I didn't care.

"I just want my notebook back." I stood up and moved toward the file folder. "It's mine. You have no right to keep it."

"It was turned over to us as evidence." Detective Morales smirked. "Voluntarily, I might add." She wrapped an arm around the file containing my notebook, and tossed a business card on the table. "I think we're through here. All of my contact information is on the card if you need anything. I'll be happy to show you out."

"Come on, Sandy," Dad said. "Let's go." He took me by the arm.

But I wasn't ready to go. Not without my notebook. I shook free of Dad's grasp. "I'm not leaving without my notebook. It's mine, and I never said you could have it." I grabbed at the file under Detective Morales' arm.

In one swift movement, Detective Morales seized my right hand with her left hand, dropped the file, and stuck her right forearm behind my left elbow nearly launching me into a front flip. "No!" I screamed and tried to twist away. But she pivoted, and forced me to the floor. My feet flew out from under me, so my forehead absorbed most of the impact. I could hear my father shouting as the darkness slowly closed in around me.

When I finally opened my eyes, I had an icepack on my forehead and a crowd of people hovering over me. "Are you okay, Sandy?" asked a faraway voice I didn't recognize. My head pounded as my eyes searched for Mom and Dad. I tried to get up.

"Just lie still now," a man said. "We're going to take you to the hospital and let them have a look at that goose egg on your forehead. "Can you wave to me with your left hand?" I waved. "How about the right one?" I waved again, this time with my right hand. "Can you move both your feet?" I must have succeeded because the man said, "Good. Very Good."

They put me on a gurney and loaded me into an ambulance. They let Mom ride with me. "Dad will meet us there," she said. The nice thing about traveling in an ambulance is that you get there quickly and you don't waste any time in the hospital waiting area, either. They wheeled me right into a little room where a nurse unhooked me from one set of tubes, and immediately hooked me up to another.

"The doctor will want a CT scan to rule out a skull fracture and intracranial hemorrhage," the nurse told Mom. You can wait here. It won't take too long."

I closed my eyes as they wheeled me back out of the room and down a hallway. "Can you hear me Sandy?" the nurse asked. I can't let you go to sleep until after the doctor has evaluated the CT scan.

I opened my eyes. "I'm tired," I whispered. I closed my eyes again.

"Sandy?" The nurse shook me a little. "Open your eyes, Sandy." She shined a flashlight into my eyes, first one and then the other. "Your pupils look good," she said. "Do you feel anything other than tired?" she asked.

"I have an awful headache." I mumbled.

"I can get you something for that," the nurse replied. "Anything else?"

"I could use about five minutes in the bathroom."

The nurse raised her eyebrows. "I can't let you off the gurney yet." Then she smiled. "Have you ever used a bedpan?"

I shook my head. "I can wait." The thought of having her place some cold pan under my butt and help me go in it was beyond embarrassing.

"There's really nothing to it, and there's no telling how long you'd have to wait. Let me warm one up for you."

I covered my eyes with the backs of my hands and braced myself for all of the humiliation that most certainly lay ahead.

I don't know what they found in the CT scan, but the doctor decided to admit me to the hospital overnight for observation. My parents didn't seem to want to talk about it. "Just get some rest now," they said. "We can talk about it later."

When I woke up, someone was in the corner of my hospital room whispering with my parents. I still felt groggy. *Very relaxed. No pain.* I strained to hear what they were talking about, but could only make out a few words here and there. I shot straight up in bed when I heard the words "involuntary commitment."

"What are you talking about?" I asked. A piercing pain shot through my head and exploded on my forehead. I reached up and felt a huge mass of flesh pulsating above my eyebrows. I lay back down and forced myself to breathe.

Mom came over to my bedside and stroked my temples. "Do you know where you are?"

"The hospital?"

Mom nodded. "Do you remember what happened?"

I tried to piece it all together. "My notebook," I said.

Mom nodded again. "Don't worry," she cooed. "We'll get your notebook back."

"But the detective . . . "

Mom patted my hand. "We won't be dealing with that detective anymore."

Dad came over by the bed, too, but he didn't say anything. They were holding my hands, but I felt myself floating away. Not back to sleep exactly—more like off to Neverland.

Neverland without Tiger Lily. I could hear the beating drums. Bam-BAM-buh, Bam-BAM-buh, Bam-BAM-buh. It sounds like a single word echoing through the forest: BeTRAYed. BeTRAYed. BeTRAYed.

I am Peter Pan. Tiger Lily betrayed me. Never again will I call on Tiger Lily. Never again will she send for Peter Pan. This is a tragedy, but I have seen many tragedies in Neverland and forgotten them all.

27

Demand me nothing. What you know, you know.
From this time forth I never will speak a word.

—*Othello*, Act V, Scene ii, Lines 303-304

I DON'T KNOW how long I slept. Doc was there when I woke up. They got me a can of Sprite and let me order some food. Once I was fully awake and settled in, Mom and Dad said we needed to talk.

"About what?" I asked.

Doc stepped forward. "About the alcohol that was in your system when you arrived at the hospital, Sandy."

My skin tingled and my hands began to shake. *Oh, yeah . . . I drank the rest of that vodka last night.* It was all coming back to me. *I wish I had some more waiting for me at home . . .*

Dad looked grim. "Where did you get it?"

I didn't answer. Instead, I closed my eyes, knowing Mom wouldn't let Dad cross-examine me at the hospital if she thought I was too tired or in pain. I reached up and ran my fingers gingerly across my forehead, wincing when I reached the bump just to add effect.

Mom jumped in to save me. "That's not important right now, Bill." She turned to me. "I want to know why you're still drinking, Sandy. What were you thinking?"

Doc shushed them both. "I would recommend that we give Sandy some space and time to reflect on those questions. My primary concern is how we keep Sandy from drinking again once the doctor signs the discharge papers tomorrow."

I wanted to tell them that was easy. I really was all out of vodka now. I wasn't going to steal anymore. I wanted nothing more to do with the police. *I'm just not cut out to be a criminal. I can't take it.* At the same time, I found myself going through lists of people who might be willing to buy more for me so I wouldn't have to steal it. *It's not like I really need it. How many weeks did I go without taking a single drink? I just want to keep a bottle around for security, to calm my nerves, just in case.* The more I thought about it the more obsessed I became with devising a fool-proof plan to get more alcohol.

I realized Doc was still talking, but I had no idea what she'd been saying. I tried to focus again on her words.

"Just a couple of days," she was saying. "We need to find the right balance and make sure you're stabilized."

"A couple of days where?" I asked, still clueless as to where this was going.

"There's a unit connected to the hospital here," said Doc. "We'll start you on a mild sedative, deal with any flashbacks, and begin to address the stressors that seem to provoke relapse."

Provoke relapse? Flashbacks? A mild sedative? I shook my head to clear my thoughts. *What had I heard them saying before?* I foraged through the fog in my mind. *Involuntary commitment. They think I'm crazy!*

I turned over onto my side, hiding my face from Doc and my parents. *They think I'm crazy. Aaron assaults me, the police attack me, my friends abandon me. Why? Because I'm crazy. I thought they were crazy, but they're all just fine. I'm the one who's crazy.*

"We don't have to decide right now," Mom said. "Let's give Sandy a chance to eat and rest and see what tomorrow brings."

"True," agreed Doc. "I would hope that we can go the voluntary route rather than involuntary, but we still have some time before Sandy's discharged."

"Food service," a voice called from the hallway.

"Bring it in," Dad answered. I could hear him shuffling papers and then pulling the bed table over to me.

"I need to go now, but I can come back this evening, Sandy," said Doc. "We can talk more then."

"Thanks, Erin," Mom said. "I'll call you if there are any changes or updates."

Dad was busy setting up my meal tray for me. "Here you go, Sandy. You'll feel better after you eat something." I ignored him.

Mom must have checked her phone. "Five messages," she said softly. "I need to make a few more calls."

"Go ahead," said Dad. "I'll stay right here until you get back."

Mom came over to the bed and kissed the side of my head before she left. "I won't be gone too long," she promised. I ignored her, too.

After several minutes of silence, Dad quietly asked if I was awake. If he thought I was asleep, he wouldn't know I was ignoring him.

"I'm awake," I garbled just loud enough to be sure he could hear me.

"Well, your food is here whenever you want it." I heard the metal hasps on his briefcase pop open. "I got you a new spiral notebook, too. And a couple of pens. I know it's not the notebook you asked for, but at least you'll have a notebook. It was the best I could find in the gift shop downstairs."

I didn't say anything. I heard him sit down in a chair by the window.

"Is there anything else I can get you?" he asked.

I really wanted to say something now, just so he'd know I wasn't trying to ignore him anymore, but I couldn't think of anything to say. Several minutes passed. I moved slightly so that I could sneak a peek at him to see what he was doing. He was leaned back with his head against the wall and his eyes closed. I waited until finally his breathing fell into the relaxed steady pattern that meant he was asleep.

I poked at my food. Three words circled in my mind, gradually moving in toward the kill: *Betrayed. Alone. Insane.* I put down my fork and picked up the notebook and one of the pens. I scribbled and crossed out and scribbled again until I'd written a poem of sorts. *It needs a title.* I wrote the question that was weighing heavy on my mind in capital letters across a clean sheet of paper:

BETTER OFF DEAD?
Betrayed
Filleted
With a blade so fine
It would surely invade
The hardest of hearts
Not only mine

Alone
I bemoan
My smart phone can't find
A place to call home
No family or friends
To ease my mind

Insane
The pain
Has me chained in bed
How long have I lain
So dazed and depressed
Out of my head

Better off dead

I did feel a little better somehow after chasing the question out of my head and onto the paper where I could examine it more closely, more objectively. The words on paper felt less threatening than the voices in my head.

Voices in your head? Doc's voice had joined the cast of characters living in my mind. *Yes, Doc, I have voices in my head, and yours is now one of them. Why should my parents pay for me to visit your office when I can visit you for free in my head?*

But you never know what I might say in real life.

True. But you never know how much of what you actually say is what I actually hear.

Sandy, sometimes I think you're just trying to mess with my mind, to keep me from messing with yours.

The best defense is a good offense, right, Doc?

You are so right.

I hear ya, Doc. When you're talking like that, I hear ya.

28

*You do surely bar the door upon your own liberty
if you deny your griefs to your friends.*

—*Hamlet*, Act III, Scene iii, Lines 352-353

WHEN DOC RETURNED that evening, she asked to talk with me alone. Mom and Dad went to get some dinner. Doc just stood at the end of my bed waiting to see if I'd say anything, I guess.

Finally, I just asked her flat out, "You think I'm crazy, don't you?"

Doc shook her head. "Not at all, Sandy. You may be the sanest kid I've ever worked with." She pointed to a chair. "Mind if I have a seat?"

"Whatever," I said. I lightly stroked the lump on my forehead. "If you don't think I'm crazy, then why do you want to put me in a nut house?"

"It's not a nut house. It's a safe place where we can get you some tools to deal with the stress of going back to school. And there are some things we need to process together before you're ready to go home with your parents."

I started fiddling with the controls on my bed. "Like what?"

"Like how to keep you from drinking."

"Well, that shouldn't be a problem. I'm really all out of vodka now," I confessed, "and I don't know how I'd get any more without breaking my promise not to steal or lie. I raised the head of my bed up as far as it could go until it was like sitting in the upright position of an airplane seat.

"I'm glad to hear you're serious about those promises you made to your parents."

I nodded. I reclined my head to about a 45 degree angle and raised up the foot of my bed. I felt like an astronaut in a space ship ready to launch. I closed my eyes. *In 5, 4, 3, 2, 1 . . . Blast off!* I opened my eyes. I wasn't going anywhere. Neither was Doc. I sighed.

"Are you experiencing any cravings or anxiety at the moment?"

"Anxiety, I guess," I reached for my forehead again. "I mean, I just got beat up by a cop who was supposed to be helping me, and now I'm stuck in a hospital bed. That makes me a little anxious."

Doc was just sitting there with her hands folded calmly in her lap. She wasn't taking any notes or anything.

"You aren't recording this, are you?" I asked.

"No, Sandy, I'm not. I just need to talk to you to get a better sense of how you're really doing."

"I'm doing just fine," I shot back.

"Are you willing to spend a couple of days here so we can do a more complete examination and have you attend some counseling sessions?" Doc asked.

I hesitated. "What kind of counseling sessions?"

"Some individual, but also some family sessions, some group sessions with other teenagers, and maybe even a session with some of your friends, just to let them know what's going on and how to help you through this difficult time."

"What friends?" I asked. I started moving the bed up and down again. Doc watched me without saying anything about it.

"Your parents suggested Troy, Cassie, Shanika, and Hector."

I shook my head. "Not Hector. And I wouldn't put Cassie and Shanika in the same room together, either, if I were you." Awkward silence. "I'm just saying . . . " I shook my head again and let the words trailed off. *What am I trying to say? That I'm not sure any of them are really my friends anymore? If they aren't . . . do I even have any friends?* I stared up at Doc.

"No problem," Doc replied. "We're not going to do anything you're uncomfortable with."

"Really?" I asked. "What if I say 'no' to the whole examination and extended stay? Are you going to let me go home?"

"I can't promise you that," Doc said. "It will be up to your parents and the psychiatrist if you don't agree to stay on your own."

"So you're just here to convince me I should stay willingly?" I could feel my red-eyed monster starting to rouse a bit. *So we can do this the easy way or the hard way. I'm sure the hard way is more interesting.* "What's in it for me if I agree?"

"Good question," Doc said.

She's just trying to buy some time. There's nothing in it for you.

"If you go voluntarily, we can put you in the step-down unit which gives you additional freedom and privileges." Doc leaned forward and pointed to the notebook on my bed table. "Have you written anything in your new notebook?"

I grabbed it instinctively.

"Your writing is a really good thing, Sandy. It seems to be both a release and a way to help you process what you're thinking and feeling." She settled back in the chair. "I got to read everything you wrote in your other notebook. It's a big part of my belief that you're really not crazy."

I clutched the notebook to my chest and thought about all the people who had read what I wrote in the other notebook. Mr. Conaway gave it to the guidance counselor; the guidance counselor gave a copy to the police; the police showed the copy to Mom, and then Mom took the notebook from me and gave it to them. *And now I'll probably never get it back.*

"Would you be willing to share what you're writing with me?" Doc asked.

I think I really am crazy. How can it be that the only person I feel like I might be able to trust right now is Erin TheRapist?

"If I show you what I'm writing, where will it end up?" I asked.

"I don't intend to share it with anyone, but since I haven't read it yet, I can't make any promises," said Doc.

"What if I told you I hear voices?" I asked.

"Depends on what kind of voices you're talking about. Do you hear them audibly or do you just hear them in your head?"

"Just in my head."

"Do you recognize the voices?"

I nodded. "Mostly Mom and Dad. Sometimes friends or teachers. I'm starting to hear your voice, now, too."

"When you hear my voice in your head, what do you hear me say?"

"You just talk to me. Sometimes you say what I want to hear. Sometimes you say what I don't want to hear."

"And your Mom's and Dad's voices?" Doc asked.

"Pretty much the same stuff they'd say if they were really there," I said.

"Have you ever thought they really were there, when they weren't?"

I shook my head and looked down. "Sometimes I've wished they were there when they weren't," I said. I looked back up. "But sometimes they were actually there, and I wished they weren't."

Doc smiled. "Sounds more like an active imagination than anything delusional."

I nodded. "Maybe so."

"Let's talk about the drinking. What happens physically if you go for more than a day without a drink?"

"I don't get withdrawal or anything." I told her. "I just get cravings when I'm feeling really stressed."

Doc nodded. "Sounds more like abuse than physical addiction. That's good." There was a long pause. "There's really only one more thing I need to ask you."

"So ask," I interjected.

Doc pursed her lips and cocked her head just a little to the right. "Do you ever feel like killing yourself?"

I took a deep breath and felt the tears coming up behind my eyes. I closed them tightly to hold back the tears. I thought about the poem in the notebook. *Would I be better off dead?* I handed my notebook to Doc.

She read the poem without saying a word. She handed the notebook back to me. "It feels like you're becoming a little freer in your writing. I'm no poet, but I think this is a good thing."

I opened the notebook and stared at my poem.

"Sandy, what do you think that poem is about?"

"Whether or not I'd be better off dead."

Doc gave me a quizzical look. "I kind of thought it was about betrayal and how you're feeling since someone betrayed you."

168

"Don't you think it means I'm suicidal?" I asked.

"Are you suicidal?" Doc countered.

I shrugged my shoulders. "How should I know? You're the doc; you tell me."

"You've asked yourself if you'd be better off dead, but have you tried to kill yourself?"

"If I had, we wouldn't be having this conversation," I retorted.

Doc nodded. "Have you ever thought about how you'd do that?"

"I'd pick something painless and very effective, that's for sure." I grabbed the bed control to lower my feet and raise my head again. "I wouldn't want to screw it up and have to face that failure on top of everything else. Especially if I left myself permanently messed up. That might be worse than dead."

Doc sighed. "Here's what I think, Sandy. You tell me if I'm wrong." She rose from her chair and stood beside me. "I don't think you're crazy or suicidal, but I do think you need a couple of days to work through some things before we send you back to school. The best place for that to happen is right here, where we know that you're safe, and we can kind of put the rest of your life on hold. Are you willing to do that?"

"I don't know." I stared out the window. It was dark out now. I wondered where my parents went to dinner and when they would be back. "It doesn't seem like it would change anything."

"Sometimes just changing the way we think about things is enough."

29

Life's but a walking shadow, a poor player
That struts and frets his hour upon the stage
And then is heard no more.

—*Macbeth*, Act V, Scene v, Lines 24-26

THE NEXT MORNING we all met with the psychiatrist. He recommended several medications, but Doc and my parents didn't seem to like any of his suggestions. I just sat there and listened to them talking about me as if I weren't there.

"I think Sandy's symptoms of depression are situational rather than chemical and have been aggravated by the alcohol," Doc said. "Every medication has its side effects, and it could take several weeks to know if it's really even helping."

Mom and Dad agreed with Doc. "Based on everything I've read, I'm afraid the potential risks outweigh the benefits in Sandy's case," Mom said. "Let's make sure we 'do no harm,' right?"

"We don't want Sandy taking any mood-altering drugs until we're sure they're absolutely necessary," Dad chimed in.

Isn't anyone going to ask me what I think? No one did.

They did decide that a private room would be better than having to deal with a roommate. The psychiatrist made a call and next thing I knew I was checking into my "special care suite." It was more like a large closet with a twin bed, a night stand, and a small dresser. Very sterile. Very white. No windows.

I don't know what I was expecting, but this place definitely wasn't Camp Disney—more like the Night of the Living Dead. The individual and family sessions weren't bad, but my first group session was frightening. We were supposed to be talking about controlling violence. No way was I going to say a word, and I tried not to make eye contact with anyone, either.

There was every kind of crazy you could imagine from cutters and druggies to anorexics and videogame freaks. Everyone looked all Goth, dressed in black and more into the violence part of the discussion than the control part. I felt like I'd fallen into an M.C. Escher painting with everything becoming more and more twisted and surreal. Or maybe it was an Ansel Adams photograph in negative form that just needed to be developed so all the black would turn white and the white would turn black and maybe a little gray to soften the stark contrasts.

I don't belong here. I don't want to be here. I looked around this room filled with strangers. Was it really all that different from school? *Where do I belong? Where do I want to be?*

I stayed completely to myself until I met Luke. I watched Luke playing foosball in the lounge and eating lunch in the cafeteria. He reminded me of someone, but I just couldn't figure out who. *Whom. Dad's voice will always be with me.* Finally, it came to me. Luke was Hermey, the misfit elf that wanted to be a dentist in *Rudolph the Red-Nosed Reindeer.* Hermey with a pierced ear and decent haircut.

We're all a bunch of misfits on the Island of Misfit Teens. Which one am I? I'd like to be the ruler, the flying lion, that reminds me of Aslan from Narnia.

I never actually talked to Luke until after the group therapy session where he got all bent out of shape for people saying "queer" instead of "gay." We were going around the circle, and we were all supposed to say one word that did NOT describe us. It was pretty interesting, with people saying things like "dead," and "perfect," and "evil." Then this guy Kevin, whose dad was a veterinarian and who had pretty much fried his brain snorting horse tranquilizers, looked right at Luke and said, "Queer!"

Luke jumped out of his chair shouting that he was gay, not queer, but Kevin insisted "queer" was the politically correct term. "They call it LGBTQ now, don't they? Lesbian, Gay, Bisexual, Transgender and Queer!"

The counselor finally had to step in and break it up. "Kevin, the 'Q' in LGBTQ actually stands for 'questioning' not 'queer.'"

"Fine," said Kevin glaring at Luke. "I'm not GAY!" But after that the whole exercise turned into a name-calling game where you stared at the person across from you and said what they were and you weren't. The counselor let "ugly" and "stupid" pass, probably because she didn't realize the new rules. The game boy looked straight at me and said, "Rich." I ignored him, but the counselor finally seemed to be catching on. When Jennifer the cutter called Karen the anorexic chick "slutty," the session ended abruptly.

Luke sat down beside me at dinner that night. "I don't care about your being rich if you don't care about my being gay," he said.

I just shrugged and shoveled a large bite of macaroni and cheese into my mouth.

Luke opened his milk carton and put in a straw. "You don't talk much, do you?"

I shrugged again, still chewing.

"I hate it here," he said. "This is the third time they've stuck me here." He opened a bag of chips and started crunching. "The first time my parents thought they could send me here and get me straightened out—as if someone could convince me I'm not really gay." Luke took a bite of his sandwich. We sat in silence as he chewed. I shoved in another spoonful of mac 'n cheese.

"The second time was after I tried to kill myself. I was really messed up that time."

I swallowed and took another big bite. I was running out of food to keep my mouth full.

"This time, I ran away. And I was doing just fine until they cancelled the credit card I took from my mom's purse."

I started taking smaller bites and chewing more slowly.

"It's okay, though. I'll have my GED by the time I turn 18, and then it won't matter anymore. I can go wherever I want to go and do whatever I want to do."

I took a long drink from my water bottle. "So where do you want to go?" I asked, breaking my code of silence.

"Austin, Texas," Luke said with a smile. "It's warm, it's affordable, and nobody cares if you're gay."

"Have you ever been there?" I asked.

"No, but I've been talking to people online, and I think that's the best place for me." He held the bag of chips up to his mouth and tapped out all of the crumbs. "That's where I was running to. But I got picked up in Arkansas."

"What will you do when you finally get to Texas?"

"Get a job," said Luke. "Maybe apply to a community college once I get my own apartment and get settled."

The cafeteria was filling up, but no one else sat down at our table.

"So what's your story?" Luke finally asked.

My story? I don't want to tell you my story. "My plan is to graduate from high school and go to Juilliard in New York City."

"What, are you a comedian?" Luke laughed as he said it.

"Maybe," I said.

"Have you been accepted?" Luke asked.

I shook my head. "I'm only a sophomore. I can't even apply for another year."

"Too bad," he replied. "A year is a really long time to have to wait. A lot can happen in a year."

I took my last bite of macaroni and wondered what all had happened to Luke in the last year. I looked around the cafeteria and wondered what had happened to all of these people over the last year. *How many are here because they really can't fit in? Are there any who just don't want to?*

I stood up. "I'm going back to my room," I said. I picked up my tray and walked away.

"See ya," Luke called after me.

Back in my room I started thinking about how long a year really was. *And I have TWO more years of high school, not just one.* Somehow, after everything I'd been through and being here, it didn't feel like I could go back to school and actually fit in any more. *I probably do belong with these misfits. At least I have the option of acting like I fit in if I want to. But do I want to? Where do I WANT to fit in?*

I stood up to do my white belt form. *I could earn my black belt over the next two years. Taekwondo. That's where I could fit in.* There was only one problem with that plan. *Shanika.* I couldn't go back to taekwondo as long as Shanika was there.

30

All things be ready, if our minds be so.

—*Henry the Fifth*, Act IV, Scene iii, Line 71

AFTER THE FIRST day, the place lost some of its "Night-of-the-Living-Dead" feel. Of course, we weren't allowed to have cell phones or internet, so that was an adjustment. Our only real connection to the outside world was a pay phone. Karen the anorexic had a boyfriend who called the pay phone 10 times a day just so she could beg him to get her out of here. I'd never used a pay phone in my life, but that was okay. There was no one I wanted to call, and I knew no one would call me.

I still didn't talk in group therapy, but no one seemed freakish anymore. We were all just trying to figure out how to make it however we could . . . fitting in, sticking out, fighting back, hiding or escaping . . . whatever worked best today. Everybody except Luke pretty much just left me alone, and Luke didn't really bother me. It was better than always being alone.

By Thursday it was time to decide for sure whether or not I was going home on Friday. Doc had talked to me a lot in individual therapy about going back to school. What to say, what not to say, and strategies for finding a safe place if I started to feel too stressed or overwhelmed. We spent a lot of time in family sessions talking about new ground rules at home and how to ask for help if and when I really felt like I needed a drink.

The biggest unresolved issue seemed to be how to reconnect with my so-called friends or how to make new friends instead. I did not want Cassie or Troy or Shanika coming to the psych ward. I finally told them I'd lied about Hector being my friend, and that he was really only Shanika's friend, not mine. I didn't mention the wrestling incident. And I just was not ready to deal with Shanika at any level, even though Mom and Dad said that Shanika called them every day to see how I was and when I would be back at school and taekwondo.

We decided that I could go home on Friday morning. My parents really wanted me to go to taekwondo on Saturday morning, but I decided I could figure out how to get out of that Saturday morning and arguing over it before I got out of the hospital might only keep me in the hospital that much longer. We also decided that once I got home, I would call Troy and see if he, and maybe even Cassie, might be willing to meet with me at Doc's office sometime over the weekend so that we could talk before I returned to school on Monday.

Saying goodbye to Luke turned out to be much harder than I'd expected. We exchanged e-mails and promised to keep in touch, but we were headed in opposite directions, and I seriously doubted our paths would ever cross again. He gave me a hug, and without really meaning to, I hugged him back. When we let go I could feel the tears in my eyes. "Break a leg, kid," Luke said.

"Mine or yours," I asked, wiping my eyes with my sleeve.

"I knew it!" Luke laughed. "You are a comedian."

Break a leg, kid. The words echoed in my head. *Kid. Why is it that everyone I want to be friends with thinks I'm just a kid?*

When I finally got home, it felt good to settle back into my own room. Mom said she needed to go to the office, but Dad stayed with me. I took a long, hot shower, put on an old sweatshirt and jeans, and then texted Troy. I let Dad read the text before I sent it. "Hi Troy, I'm home. Please call me. Your friend, Sandy." I thought the "your friend" thing sounded a little cheesy, but Dad liked the idea of letting him know that I was reaching out as a friend to kind of break the ice or set the tone or whatever, so I added it.

Dad made us some lunch. I was really happy to be home from a food standpoint. I had been eating cold cereal for breakfast each morning and nothing but macaroni and cheese for my other meals because that was the only thing that even looked edible to me. *Rich kid,* the game boy's voice muttered in my mind. *No, I just happen to have taste.*

After lunch Dad asked if I wanted to watch a movie. "Let's watch *Rudolph the Red-Nosed Reindeer*," I suggested.

"The Christmas DVD?" Dad asked. "Are you serious?"

I nodded. "You dig it out while I make popcorn."

Dad didn't argue with me. At first I could tell he was watching me instead of the show, though. When Hermey appeared, I jumped off the couch and pointed to the TV. "There!" I shouted. "Doesn't Hermey look just like Luke?"

Dad laughed. "The resemblance is uncanny," he admitted. After that he relaxed and watched the rest of the show with me. When it was over, he asked me if I was feeling like a misfit.

"Maybe," I answered. "I mean, I think I can fit in when I want to. I'm just not sure anymore where I want to fit in."

Dad sighed. "It amazes me how far ahead you seem to be from most of my sophomores in college . . . and you, still a sophomore in high school." He gave me a hug. "I love you, Sandy," he whispered. "You fit in our family just fine."

We were looking through the other Christmas DVD's and Dad was trying to convince me that we should watch *It's a Wonderful Life* next, when Mom called.

"Fine," Dad said to her. Then, "okay" and "How long?" The only other thing I heard before he hung up was, "we will," and "I love you, too."

"She's on her way home," Dad told me.

"Does she want to watch *It's a Wonderful Life*, too?"

"No," Dad replied. "She's bringing a visitor for you."

"A visitor for me?" I looked at my watch. Troy and Cassie would still be in school. Shanika might not, though, since she worked for her dad in the afternoons. I closed my eyes. *Please don't let it be Shanika.*

Dad came and sat beside me on the couch. "Sandy?" he asked. "Are you okay?" He waited.

"Who's coming?" I asked as evenly as possible.

"I think your mom kind of wanted it to be a surprise, but maybe we're better off with no surprises."

"No surprises," I agreed.

"It's Don Goldman," Dad said quietly. He watched me carefully as he said it.

"The District Attorney?" I asked. "Why is the D.A. coming to our house?"

"Your mom said he wants to talk to you," Dad replied.

"Why would he want to talk to me?" I stuffed the last handful of popcorn into my mouth.

"I'm not really sure," said Dad. "The cynical side of me thinks he wants to make sure we don't sue the detective for police brutality. Or maybe it's a professional courtesy he's extending to your mom." He started packing up the Christmas videos to put them back in storage. "I guess we'll know soon enough."

"I'll be right back," I said. I went upstairs to my bathroom to examine my forehead. The lump was nearly gone, but the bruise was still a deep purple. There weren't any mirrors in the psych ward, so I really hadn't looked at myself all week. I splashed cold water on my face, patted it dry with a towel, and then stared at myself again. *I'm still not sure if I like what I see. But I'm tired of feeling afraid, and I'm done hiding. Bring it on.*

I stepped away from the mirror, stood at attention, bowed, and recited my taekwondo pledge to no one but myself. Then I went to my room and went through all of the orange belt steps I know. I was in the middle of white belt form when I heard the garage door opening. I finished the form, and was through two of the three sparring steps when I heard someone coming up the stairs.

I'd left my door open, but Mom knocked anyway.

"How are you doing?" she asked. I nodded, and she came in. She hugged me, and softly kissed the bruise on my forehead before letting go. "Don Goldman is here with me," she said. "You remember Don?"

I nodded. He and his wife had been to dinner at our house before he was the elected prosecutor. He and Mom both graduated from Duke Law School, and she had supported him in his campaign. "Why is he here?" I asked.

"He just wants to talk to you," Mom said. "And I think he has something for you."

When we came downstairs, Dad and Mr. Goldman were sitting at the dining room table. Mr. Goldman stood and held out his hand when I walked in. "Hi, Sandy," he said. "It's so good to see you again." He was even taller than I remembered with dark curly hair and blue eyes that seemed to see right through all false pretenses. He waited until I sat down before sitting back in his chair. "I thought you were great in the musical last week," he said. "You probably know my niece Grace. She was one of the lost boys."

"Thank you," I said in exactly the good-manner voice my parents had taught me to use when someone paid me a compliment. "I didn't know Grace was your niece."

He nodded. "My sister's daughter. She was thrilled to actually get a part as a freshman. Great program Hamilton runs there at the school." His voice trailed off. He cleared his throat and reached for his briefcase. "I have something for you," he said, placing his briefcase on the table and popping it open. He handed me the notebook the police had taken from me. "I believe this is yours."

"Thank you," I said again, using the same good-manner voice. I tried to figure out what this was supposed to mean. "You don't need it anymore?" I asked.

Mr. Goldman shook his head. He pulled a file from his briefcase and set it on the table. Then he closed the briefcase and put it back on the floor beside his chair. He laid both of his palms flat on the file in front of him and looked me directly in the eyes. "First, let me tell you how really sorry I am that this happened to you. I'm sorry that Aaron Jackson assaulted you, and I'm sorry that Detective Morales gave you that nasty bruise on your forehead."

I felt my ears burning and resisted the urge to reach up and touch the bruise.

"You didn't deserve any of this. I want you to know that I have read all of the reports, and I absolutely believe that you told the police the truth, and I really wish there were something I could do to make this all right." He shifted uncomfortably in his chair and pulled a stack of papers out of the file. He handed them to Mom.

"These are the reports the Detective sent to my office for charging purposes. I promised you copies, and here they are."

I could see Mom clenching her teeth as she looked through them. "Theft . . . Minor in Possession of Alcohol . . . Obstructing Justice . . . Perjury . . . Resisting Law Enforcement . . . Battery to a Police Officer . . . " She shook her head angrily. "Some of these are felonies!" Mom exclaimed. She shuffled through the papers again. "Did I miss anything?"

"No," Mr. Goldman replied. "That's all six charges the detective submitted against Sandy."

Dad pounded his fist on the table. "You think Sandy is the criminal here?"

Mom held Dad's arm and tried to quiet him. "Don knows Sandy is not a criminal. He wouldn't be here if he thought that."

Mr. Goldman nodded. "Sandy's definitely not the criminal here. I won't be filing any of these charges. I know the sergeant had Detective Morales prepare these reports just to cover her own butt and protect the police department." He took a deep breath, and Dad did the same. "I don't agree with it, but I also know the detective was probably within the department's reasonable force continuum guidelines when someone tries to take evidence from a detective."

Dad didn't look happy about this last statement. "So why are you really here?" he asked accusingly. "Just to make sure we don't sue the police department?"

Mr. Goldman shook his head. "My primary purpose in coming here personally was to explain to Sandy why I won't be filing any criminal charges against Aaron Jackson, even though I have absolutely no doubt that Aaron committed a B felony sexual assault and deserves to spend the next 10 to 20 years in prison. I firmly believe that our community would be safer if Aaron Jackson were registered as a violent sex offender."

"If you know he did it, why don't you charge him?" Dad asked. "And you can charge him for raping Shanika Washington, too, while you're at it."

"I'd love to, Bill. I have probable cause for both charges, but I don't believe there is any way at all I could get a conviction on either count. I don't mind filing a long shot and letting the chips fall where they may, but I think if I tried this to 100 juries, I'd lose 100 times." He looked at Mom to see if she agreed. She nodded. "I can't justify the expense to the taxpayers, and I can't believe you'd want to put Sandy through that either."

"Sometimes it's better to just move on," Mom said. She looked at me and raised her eyebrows inquiringly. "What do you think, Sandy?"

I was thinking about Aaron actually raping Shanika. I was wondering why she didn't tell me that herself. I was gathering that Mr. Goldman did not intend to file any criminal charges of any kind against Aaron, and that's why he was giving me my notebook back. Mom seemed to think this was for the best. Dad wasn't happy about it.

"I don't know," I replied weakly. "I don't know what I'm supposed to think anymore."

31

Choose your own company, and command what cost
Your heart has mind to.

—*Antony and Cleopatra*, Act III, Scene iv, Lines 37-38

TROY CALLED JUST as Mr. Goldman was leaving. "Hey, Sandy," he said. "I got your message. How are you doing?"

"Better," I said. "I have a huge bruise on my forehead from where the detective threw me to the floor, but aside from that, I'm good."

"So is that why you were in the hospital?"

"Yeah," I said. "I had a concussion, so they wanted to observe me for a few days."

"So how'd you get crosswise with a detective?"

"I just wanted my notebook back. Trying to grab it from a police officer wasn't a very bright decision on my part, though."

"So did you get it back?" Troy asked.

"I did, so I guess all's well that ends well, right?"

"I guess," agreed Troy.

After a moment of silence, I decided it was time to launch into the little speech I'd practiced with Doc. "I've been going through a lot lately, and I've really missed you. Mom and Dad have sent me to a counselor, and I want to talk with you about everything that's happened, but I'm still feeling a little afraid." I took a deep breath. Troy didn't say anything. I wondered if he was still there. "Anyway, I was hoping that you'd be willing to meet with me and my counselor so I can tell you about what I've been going through."

"You want me to meet with you and your counselor?" Troy asked.

"Yes." I said.

"When?" asked Troy.

"Sometime this weekend," I replied. "Any time before I have to go back to school on Monday."

"What about Cassie?"

"I was going to call her next."

"Can we both come at the same time?"

"Sure," I said. "I'd like that."

"I'm pretty sure she has a date with Aaron tonight. What about tomorrow morning? Not too early, like maybe 10:30?"

"Let me check with Doc," I said, "but I think that should work. Do you mind meeting me downtown at her office?"

"I can do that. Text me the address as soon as we hang up, okay?"

"You got it. And Troy . . . " I hesitated and had to swallow hard. "Thanks. I really appreciate this."

"No problem," said Troy. "It's been pretty weird without you lately."

I let Mom and Dad know that I'd talked to Troy, and we confirmed the time with Doc. "Are you ready to call Cassie?" Mom asked. "Do you want me or your Dad to make the call for you?"

Just when I was thinking things with Cassie couldn't possibly get any worse. A call from my parents now, and she'll write me off forever. I shook my head and took a deep breath.

"Thanks, Mom," I said, "but I think this is something I really need to do myself."

"All right," said Mom. "Just let me know as soon as you hang up."

"I don't even know if she'll answer. I'll probably just get her voice mail." I went up to my room and tried to collect myself. I prayed that if Cassie did answer, she wouldn't be with Aaron. I dialed the number and tried to relax. Things with Troy had been okay, so maybe Cassie would be ready to listen now, too.

She answered. Her "hello" sounded edgy, icy. I wanted to hang up, but she knew it was me from her caller ID.

"Hey, Cassie," I said. "It's me, Sandy."

"Hey yourself," she said. "Troy told me you'd probably be calling."

"Oh, good," I said, trying to act happy about the fact that Troy called her the second he hung up with me. "Did he tell you what's going on?"

"He told me you want us to meet with you and your shrink tomorrow morning at 10:30."

"Would that be okay with you?" I didn't wait for an answer. "I've been going through a lot lately, and I've really missed you. I need to talk to you and Troy. Mom and Dad have sent me to this counselor, and, well, I just talked with Troy…"

"Is this about Aaron?" Cassie cut me off. "He told me you and Shanika Washington are both crazy. Are you ready to tell the truth now?"

My hands were shaking so hard I could barely hold the phone to my ear. I sat down on the edge of my bed and leaned forward as far as I could. Far enough to keep me from saying a word.

"Are you ready to drop your stupid story about Aaron assaulting you?" Cassie insisted. The way she said it made me think that Aaron was right there with her listening to every word we were saying.

I sat up straight and took a deep breath. "The truth is Aaron sexually assaulted me," I said, my voice just above a whisper.

No response.

"Cassie?"

"I don't believe it." Her voice was curt now. "Why are you doing this?"

"Just forget it," I said.

There was a muffled sound, like Cassie was covering the phone and whispering to someone else.

"See you around," I said.

"Not if I see you first," she retorted, and I could hear Aaron laughing in the background as she hung up.

I was giving Mom and Dad the gist of my conversation with Cassie when Troy called me back.

I answered tentatively. "Hello?"

"Hey, Sandy."

"Hey, Troy."

"Um, I'm really sorry, but I'm not going to be able to make it tomorrow after all."

"You could come without Cassie, you know," I said.

"Don't make me choose between you and Cassie," Troy pleaded.

"I'm not the one making you choose," I said. "She is."

"I want to be there for you, Sandy, but I HAVE to be there for Cassie."

"What about Aaron?" I asked.

"Aaron won't be around forever," said Troy. "He doesn't love her."

"So you're just going to spend your life waiting in the wings?"

"It's not like that," Troy said. "Think about it. Let's say Cassie's right and you're blowing whatever happened with Aaron all out of proportion. Then it's better that I don't go tomorrow. On the other hand, let's say you're telling the truth, and Aaron is as much of a creep as I think he is. He's going to do a serious number on Cassie, and I need to be there for her when he does. Either way, Cassie needs me to be there for her."

There was no point in arguing with Troy's logic. Part of me was relieved not to have to face either of them tomorrow, until the reality began setting in that our friendship was really over.

"Sandy? Are you there?"

"I understand," I said. "Maybe I'll see you around."

"I hope so, Sandy," Troy sounded truly torn. "I really hope so."

I hung up and turned to face Mom and Dad. "Troy's not coming tomorrow either," I said.

"Oh, Sandy." My mom came over and gave me a big hug. "I'm so sorry."

"It's okay," I lied. "I'm not really surprised."

"Well, I am," Dad said. "You three have been best friends your whole life, and when you need them most, they completely abandon you."

"I guess we may as well call Doc back and cancel the 10:30 appointment," I said.

Mom and Dad exchanged a glance. "Come and sit with me on the couch for a minute," Mom said to me. "I want to talk to you about something."

I didn't have a good feeling about whatever it was Mom wanted to say, but I very reluctantly let her lead me to the couch. "What is it?" I asked.

"I want to talk to you about Shanika," Mom began.

"What about Shanika?" I was disappointed with Cassie and Troy, but that was nothing compared to the fury I felt when Shanika's name crossed my lips.

"She's called the house every day. She really wants to talk to you. Why don't we call Shanika and see if she'd keep the 10:30 appointment with you?"

"I don't have anything to say to Shanika," I said. "And anyway, she probably has to teach taekwondo tomorrow."

Dad came over to where we were sitting. "Well, I think Shanika really wants to talk to you, even if you don't have anything to say to her." Dad put his hand on my shoulder. "It wouldn't hurt to call her and ask."

"And we can change the time if we need to," Mom added.

"Fine," I said. I stood up. "You call Shanika. You set it up. You drive me there, and we'll just see what happens. I'll be in my room."

32

This above all: To thine own self be true.

—*Hamlet*, Act I, Scene iii, Line 78

I SAT ON my bed and read through the spiral notebook that Mr. Goldman had returned to me. I pulled out the new notebook Dad bought for me and copied my *Better Off Dead* poem into the old one. I wished that I could write another poem to figure out how I was feeling now, but nothing was coming. *Maybe if I had a drink . . .* But I didn't really want a drink, which was good, because I didn't have anything to drink anyway. Plus, my parents would be monitoring that pretty closely.

Maybe there wasn't a word in English that described my feelings. *Maybe no one else has ever felt this way. Maybe I should make up a word that describes this feeling.* I sneaked downstairs and borrowed Dad's Latin Dictionary. *If I'm going to make up a word, best to start with a solid Latin root.*

I flipped through the dictionary until the restlessness and futility consumed me. I tossed the book on the bed and ran through my taekwondo forms a couple of times. When I lay back down on the bed, I pulled out the old notebook and opened to a clean page. I wrote "Friends" on the top left side and "Enemies" on the top right side. I wrote "Aaron" under "Enemies." I wrote "Luke" under "Friends." I wondered when Luke would be getting out of the psych ward. I couldn't bring myself to write Troy or Cassie or Shanika on either side. I tore out the page, wadded it up, and threw it in the trash can.

When Mom called me down for dinner, I was very happy to have another nice, home-cooked meal.

"It's supposed to be 60 degrees and sunny tomorrow afternoon," Dad said. "I thought I'd get the bicycles all tuned up tomorrow morning so we can go for a bike ride later in the day."

"That sounds good," Mom said. "Would you like that, Sandy?"

"Sure," I said. "Let's ride up to the old Coney dog place. I can't remember the last time I had a root beer float."

Dad smiled. He was swirling a glass of ice water in his hand, the way he would normally swirl a glass of red wine with the meal. It seemed strange to me that my parents were not drinking wine with the meal, but I didn't say anything about it. Doc had suggested at one of our family sessions that they completely remove all alcoholic beverages from the house and not drink in front of me for the time being. She said just seeing or smelling the alcohol could be a trigger for me. I think the real reason they got rid of everything was to make sure I couldn't sneak into it when they were sleeping.

Dad cleared his throat and raised his eyebrows at Mom.

"Sandy, did you have any questions about the things Don was saying when he visited this afternoon?"

"Not really," I said. *Just because you tell them doesn't mean they'll do anything about it. Shanika's voice.* I thought back to the day we sat in her car and I told her about Aaron. She talked about hazing and she even said something about "the rape." I remember how funny

I felt when she said "rape." *Why didn't she tell me about what Aaron did to her right then? Why did she tell me about Hector and the wrestling team, but not about her and Aaron? She thinks I'm just a kid, that's why. I'm only a sophomore, a taekwondo student. I was crazy to think I was her friend.*

"Sandy?" Mom touched my arm. "Did you hear me?"

"Sorry, Mom," I apologized. "What were you saying?"

"I was saying that I'll take you to Doc's tomorrow morning and do some work at my office while you and Shanika talk with Doc. You can call me when you're ready for me to pick you up."

"So you talked to Shanika?" I asked.

"I did," Mom said. "She said her Dad would cover her classes tomorrow. She'll be there at 10:30."

"Did she say anything else?" I asked. I drained my water glass, wiped my mouth, and folded my napkin up beside my plate.

"Just that she's really glad you're home and doing better and how much she really wants to talk to you tomorrow," Mom said.

"Well, I'm glad it worked out for her to go," said Dad.

"How are you feeling about seeing Shanika tomorrow?" Mom asked.

"I don't know," I said. *Angry. Scared. Anxious. Nervous. Excited. Why did Shanika agree to this? Did Mom push her into it?* I blinked several times to clear my eyes and my thoughts. "I'm glad Doc will be there. I don't think I could do it otherwise." I could feel Mom and Dad both looking at me.

"It'll be fine," Dad said.

I suddenly wanted out—out of my meeting with Shanika and Doc and out of this conversation. "I think I'd like to get started on the homework assignments you picked up for me." I carried my plate and glass to the kitchen sink. "I don't want to be too far behind when I go back to school on Monday." I picked up the stack of school books sitting on the counter. "Do you mind if I work in my room?"

"Go ahead," said Dad.

"Come back down if you need a study break or a snack," Mom called after me. "I baked some brownies, and there's ice cream in the freezer."

I lumbered up the steps, taking two at a time. When I reached my room I dropped all of the books on my bed. English, Biology, World History . . . lots of reading to do. On top of the stack was a copy of *Anthem* by Ayn Rand. I picked up the assignment sheet. "Hi Sandy, We're reading *Anthem* and discussing the importance of thinking for yourself rather than succumbing to peer pressure. This week we wrote a factual newspaper article about Equality 7-2521's escape from jail, his surprise appearance at the World Council of Scholars, and his flight into the Uncharted Forest. The assignment due next week is to write an opinionated editorial about the same events, written by one of the Scholars. You can turn them both in at the same time."

Friday night. Cassie is out with Aaron. Troy is probably working on some car in his uncle's garage. Shanika's at the studio teaching taekwondo classes. Am I going to sit at home doing homework? Guess so. I thought of Luke. *At least I'm not stuck in the psych ward.* So I spent my Friday night reading *Anthem*. It was a really quick read—so weird at first because everything was plural: "we" instead of "I" and "they" instead of "he" or "she." It's all about some post-apocalypse society where there's no individuality or creativity of any kind allowed. It made me think.

Is it more important to fit in or to be myself? I pulled out my notebook and wrote the words swirling through my mind: *Conformity. Uniformity. Equality. Individuality. Creativity. Diversity. Unity. Integrity. Re-*

sponsibility. *So many "ity"-bitty words swirling through my mind. What do any of them really mean?* I thought about my meeting with Doc and Shanika the next morning. *Insanity. Intensity. Complexity. Seniority. I wish I were a senior, too. Maybe then Shanika would want me for a friend.* I searched again in Dad's Latin book for the right words to express what I was feeling about Shanika. I came up with this phrase: *Communicare Complexus. Like it's just too complicated to communicate.* I started writing:

> *I have this feeling.*
> *Somewhere in the universe there must be a word.*
> *A word attached solely to this feeling alone.*
> *A word that I could say, that you would hear,*
> *Allowing us both to understand.*
>
> *If such a word exists, it eludes me.*
>
> *I've considered creating the word myself . . .*
> *but how would I explain its meaning*
> *to you?*

I stopped writing and closed my notebook. I buried my face in my pillow, hoping to smother myself and wondering how many tears you have to cry to actually drown in them.

Mom woke me up at 9:30 Saturday morning. I ate my bagel and drank my orange juice in silence. Part of me wanted to see Shanika more than anything in the world, while another part of me never wanted to see Shanika again. *Which part is really me?*

I found myself thinking about this six-word paragraph I read in *Anthem*: "I am. I think. I will." The words were so powerful, but they kept turning into questions in my mind. *I am. Who am I? I think. What do I think? I will. I will what? Maybe I will, but maybe I won't. Maybe I will, but maybe I don't. Maybe I don't will anything. Maybe it all happens regardless of my will.*

Dad walked into the kitchen and poured himself a cup of coffee. He was wearing the bike shorts Mom got him for Christmas. They were supposed to be baggy, but they looked pretty snug to me, especially after months of seeing him in sweats. He kissed Mom. "Can't wait to break in the new shorts. Check out all of these pockets." He unzipped the leg pockets and then zipped them up again, stuck his hands in the side pockets, and then whirled around to show off the back zip pocket that was supposed to be hidden.

"Looking good," Mom said with a smile.

Dad came over and rested both hands on my shoulders. "I'll have all the bikes in good shape by the time you two get back. Are you ready to ride this afternoon, Sandy?"

"I am," I said.

33

For they breathe truth that breathe their words in pain.

—*Richard II*, Act II, Scene i, Line 8

MOM DROPPED ME off in front of Doc's office building. "Do you want me to come in with you?"

"Mom . . . " I searched for words. *I'm not a little kid anymore. You can't hold my hand forever.* I just shook my head. "I'll be okay."

"Just call me if you need me or whenever you're ready."

I walked into Doc's waiting area. No sign of Shanika. *Maybe she won't come after all.* I rang the buzzer to let Doc know I was there. She came out and motioned for me to have a seat beside her in the lobby.

"How are you doing this morning?" she asked.

"I'm okay."

"I am really pleased that you are here and willing to talk with Shanika," she said.

I shrugged. "I'm not even sure she'll really come."

"Sandy," Doc said gently, "Shanika is already here. She was feeling a little nervous and asked if she could come early. Shanika was afraid you might not come."

"It's not like my Mom gave me a choice."

"I'm giving you the choice now," said Doc. "Do you want to talk with Shanika?"

I got up from the chair and paced back and forth. Doc let me pace for several minutes.

"Sandy?" Doc said finally.

I stopped. "What's the point?" I turned to face Doc, but no other words would come.

"It's up to you," Doc replied.

"I don't have anything to say."

"Then you don't have to say anything," Doc reassured me. "Are you willing to listen?"

I sat down again beside Doc. "Do you know what she's going to say?"

"I have an idea, but I'm not sure Shanika really knows exactly what she'll say once she sees you." I was staring at the floor. Doc waited until I looked up and she could catch my eye. "I believe Shanika's here because she really cares about you."

I laughed. "You mean like a big sister? Or my taekwondo instructor making the extra effort to see if she can help?" I shook my head. "She's done enough, thank you very much."

"It's up to you," Doc said again. "You are free to leave, or I can ask Shanika to leave, and you and I can keep the appointment without her."

I sat with my arms crossed, bouncing my right leg. I kept waiting for Doc to tell me what to do, so I could just refuse. Or if I did what she told me and still failed, it would be her fault for telling me to do it, not mine. But that's not how Doc worked.

"You asked me a minute ago what the point is." Doc continued to sit there all calm and collected. "One of the things that seem to be working well for you right now is taekwondo. You might be able to avoid Shanika at school, but what about taekwondo?"

I sighed and slowly raised myself out of the chair. "Let's just get it over with," I conceded.

Doc led me back to her office where Shanika was sitting on the loveseat. "Have a seat, Sandy."

Shanika stood up. "Hi, Sandy." I kept my distance and decided it would be best to have the table between us. I picked a chair at the far side of the table. I expected Doc to sit in the chair next to Shanika, but she didn't. She sat down behind her desk and gave Shanika an encouraging nod.

Shanika sat back down, this time in the chair next to the loveseat. "I guess you probably feel pretty mad at me right now," she began.

I could feel her eyes pleading with me to look at her, but I fixed my gaze on the table.

"I'm pretty mad at me, too, so I really don't blame you." Shanika came over and sat down at the table across from me. She tried to put her face in my line of vision, but I turned away. She reached out her hand and touched mine. "Sandy, I'm sorry," she said.

I pulled my hand away. I wanted to look at her, but tears were flooding my eyes.

"I never meant to hurt you, and I really am sorry." Shanika whispered.

Doc walked over with a box of tissues, put them on the table between us, and joined us at the table. We both looked at her. She handed us each a tissue. I blotted my eyes, but still didn't say anything.

"Is there anything else you want to say, Shanika?" Doc asked quietly.

Shanika grabbed another tissue from the box and blew her nose. She took a deep breath before answering, "Just that I hope Sandy can forgive me and that we can still be friends."

"Sandy," Doc said quietly, "is there anything you would like to ask Shanika about what she's said?"

My emotions scampered furiously about like a hamster in one of those little plastic exercise balls. I was as dizzy as if my body were physically spinning right along with my emotions. *Shanika still wants to be friends. Don't blow this.* I leaned back in my chair to regain my balance and tried to sneak a peek at Shanika, but lost my nerve. I took a deep breath and told Doc, "I want to know why she didn't tell me herself before . . . why . . . if I was her friend . . . why I had to hear about her and Aaron from the police."

"I wanted to tell you, Sandy!" cried Shanika. "Honest, I did. I tried about a million different ways to tell you in my head, but it seemed like it would only make things worse." Shanika was up walking around now. She paced as she talked. "But you're right. I should have told you. I wish I had told you."

"But you didn't," I said still staring at the table.

"I was afraid," admitted Shanika.

I looked into her eyes for the first time in a week. The bright excitement that had shone last Saturday was gone. All I saw now was pain. *Whose pain? Is it her pain I'm seeing or just a reflection of my own?* I finally forced my mouth to form the words, "You were afraid of me?"

Shanika started to nod, but then shook her head instead. "Not afraid of you—just afraid you wouldn't respect me anymore."

"Like whatever Aaron did to you was your fault?" I asked.

Shanika winced at Aaron's name. "I did date him, Sandy. I wanted to go out with him." She sank into the chair next to the loveseat. "He was cool and popular. I was all excited that he liked me." She buried her face in her hands and said something else I couldn't quite make out. She leaned back in the chair and exhaled deeply. "I never imagined he would be like that."

Part of me wanted to make Shanika tell me every sordid detail of what Aaron did to her, but I'd read the police report. I already had a pretty good idea. The police had grilled her just like they'd grilled me. And in the end, they hadn't believed either one of us.

"I believe you," I whispered. "I believe you."

We were all silent until Doc asked me, "Is there anything else that you'd like to ask or share?"

I shrugged, not having a clue where to go from here.

"Do you still want to be friends with Shanika?" Doc asked, her voice leading me tenderly toward the answer in my heart.

I nodded.

Doc turned to Shanika. "How about you, Shanika? How do you feel about your friendship with Sandy?"

What Shanika said next totally blew me away. "Except for my family," she began, "I've never cared about anybody as much as I care about Sandy."

We talked with Doc about what we each expected from the friendship and how this would work at school and taekwondo. Finally, I felt ready to move forward. "Do you think it would it be okay if Shanika drove me home?" I asked Doc.

Shanika's eyes lit up and she smiled broadly. "You got it!" Shanika exclaimed. But then she hesitated and looked at Doc.

Doc nodded. "Sandy, why don't you call your mom and clear it with her."

It felt so good to be sliding into the passenger side of Shanika's car. After we were both buckled in, she said, "That is one nasty bruise on your forehead. Does it still hurt?"

"Not so much anymore."

"Well, you look like you've been trying to break bricks with your head!"

"At least I waited until after the musical to do it." I laughed. "Lucky for me I've got such a thick skull."

"You are lucky alright," Shanika shot back with a grin. "If you'd stuck me with that understudy Gavin the Lost Boy, your butt would be even more bruised than your head!"

34

'Tis in ourselves that we are thus or thus. Our bodies are gardens, to the which our wills are gardeners. So that if we will plant nettles or sow lettuce, set hyssop and weed up thyme, supply it with one gender of herbs or distract it with many, either to have it sterile with idleness or manured with industry—why, the power and corrigible authority of this lies in our wills.

—*Othello*, Act I, Scene iii, Line 8

WHEN I RETURNED to school on Monday, somebody had been spreading the rumor that I really thought I was Peter Pan and had cracked my head open trying to fly. Lots of people commented on the big bruise, but no one ever asked me how I really got it. I saw Troy a couple of times across the lunchroom, but he avoided making eye contact each time. Cassie must have always seen me first, because I didn't see her or Aaron at all.

The last few weeks of school passed quickly. I had been attending practically every taekwondo class offered, and Shanika invited me to her graduation party. Her plan was to study business and communications at the university where Dad taught so she could still live at home and teach taekwondo classes.

"Someday I'll own this and a dozen other do-jahngs," she told me.

"Do you think you'll sign up for any of my dad's literature classes?" I asked.

Shanika laughed. "If I do, I'll have to hire you as a tutor!"

"Whoever heard of a college student hiring a high school student to tutor her?"

"Exactly," said Shanika. So I guess she planned to avoid Dad's classes as much as possible.

The summer youth theater program would fill up most of the month of July for me, but Mom's firm hired me to work part-time as an office gopher for the time I was free in June and August. So I started riding in to work with Mom in the mornings, but then Shanika would pick me up after lunch and I'd spend the afternoons hanging out with her at the do-jahng, taking classes or just helping out.

One night we stayed late so Shanika could work on her weapons routine for the world competitions. Shanika had picked a fast-moving song with a powerful beat for her performance. After she'd practiced her forms and freestyle, she put her weapons away and turned on some music that sounded like a dance club mix. "Free-style!" she shouted and began dancing all around me.

"Come on shake your body. Sandy, shake your body," she chanted as she pranced and twirled. She pulled me along with her, and I tried to follow her lead, imitating whatever moves I could and ignoring the rest. Shanika whipped around and tried to bump hips with me. "Come on bump your boo-tay. Sandy, bump your boo-tay." We danced and bumped until we finally collapsed in the middle of the floor laughing hysterically.

I lay flat on my back, knees up, chest heaving from the exhilarating work-out.

"Now that's what I call dancing!" Shanika exclaimed. She was lying on her side, head propped on one hand supported by an elbow.

I rolled over on my side and propped my head up to face her. When our eyes met, I felt something click inside me, connecting me to Shanika forever. I sat up, but I still couldn't take my eyes from Shanika. Her nose and forehead glistened with beads of sweat, but she looked absolutely beautiful. So full of energy, and so full of life. A wave of warm excitement washed over my body. Shanika and I were suddenly suspended in time. There was no past and no future, just the two of us together in that present moment.

"You're trembling," Shanika said. She reached out and took my hand in hers. I had no idea how cold I was until I felt the warmth of her hands. I felt a treasure chest of butterflies opening inside me, their wings fluttering freely about in my stomach.

Shanika's smile captured my gaze and I watched her lips form my name. "Sandy?"

I couldn't take my eyes from her lips. I felt my own lips part ever so slightly as I drew in a taste of the air around us. I savored the breath that Shanika exhaled as my lungs slowly filled. Every breath seemed to draw us closer together.

Shanika leaned in close to my ear and whispered, "Have you ever wondered what it would be like to kiss me?"

The electricity of this idea sent a tingling sensation throughout my body. I breathed in deeply and our eyes locked.

"You mean before right now?" I asked. I tried to blink back my surprise.

Shanika nodded.

I shook my head. "Have you ever thought about kissing me?" I asked.

Shanika's lips spread out across her face into the biggest grin I'd ever seen. She nodded, still holding my gaze. "Only about a hundred times."

I bit my lower lip. "How come I never knew that?"

"I was afraid. I wouldn't want to risk our friendship."

We were both whispering now, our faces so close that our noses nearly touched.

Shanika turned her head ever so slightly. "You can kiss me now if you want."

I smiled and closed my eyes. *Maybe I will.*

Author's Note

Many readers will ask whether Sandy is short for Sanford or Sandra. My answer is "Yes." Some readers will identify strongly with Sandy as exclusively male or female, while others will read the book twice, once assuming Sandy is one gender and again assuming the opposite gender. In discussions, some will use the masculine pronouns and some will use the feminine. Others will undertake the cumbersome task of using both disjunctively (he or she, his or her), and some may attempt an entirely gender neutral commentary. Do whatever is most comfortable for you. I am not an advocate for gender neutrality. Instead, I believe we're moving toward becoming a society that embraces and values male and female experiences equally, and I hope that *Maybe I Will* is a step in that direction.

About the Author

Laurie Gray has worked as a high school teacher, a deputy prosecuting attorney, and the founder of Socratic Parenting LLC (www.SocraticParenting.com). In addition to writing, speaking and consulting, Laurie currently works as a bilingual child forensic interviewer at her local child advocacy center and as an adjunct professor of criminal sciences at Indiana Tech University. She has served on the faculty of the National Symposium for Child Abuse in Huntsville, Alabama, annually since 2009. Her debut novel *Summer Sanctuary* (Luminis Books, 2010) received a Moonbeam Gold Medal for excellence in young adult fiction and was named a 2011 Indiana Best Book Finalist. Her third young adult novel, *Just Myrto* (Luminis Books, 2014) will carry readers back to ancient Greece to meet Socrates, Laurie's favorite teacher of all time.